STORIES

told among the Mockingbirds

STORIES

told among the Mockingbirds

JOYCE BURNS

ISBN: Softcover 6x9 978-0-9887390-3-1
ISBN: Hardcover 978-0-9887390-4- 8
ISBN: E-book 978-0-9887390-2- 4

For permission requests, contact:
Joyce Burns
Chyna Blues Press
138 Cliff West Rd.
Tupelo, Ms. 38801
chynablues13@gmail.com

First Edition, January 2026, ©Joyce Burns,
Chyna Blues Press
Book Cover design, Interior design, art and photos
by Joyce Burns

This book was printed in the United States of America

www.chynablues.com

Dedication

This book is dedicated to my brother Ronnie Hill, my hero, who truly was the wind beneath my wings; and to his renegade band of gypsies and their creative abilities. Thank you for being a part of my life. I will love you for eternity.

In particular, to James Alvin Moore, Paul Dulaney, Daniel Dulaney, Jerry Rickles, Don Nerren, and Billy Roberson.

Also, to my loving family who encouraged my creativity and were always there for every joy and tear. God knows how they got us grown, but what an absolutely magnificent childhood

And thanks to my friend K.L. Estes for his support and inspiration. To Cecil Cheek who was always there for us, and to Mitzi Moore for inspiring me long, long ago.

Joyce Burns -Author

"You can kid the world. But not your sister."

- Charlotte Gray

Table of Contents

Other Fiction

Introduction

From the day I was born, on a blustery day in April, in the small town of New Albany, Mississippi, my brother Ronnie always said that I was his lucky penny, as he felt I had brought him luck on that day. As the story goes, he was picked up at school that day to come see his new baby sister, and didn't have to ride the bus home from school. The bus that day, crashed on its route and a lot of kids were injured, some of them seriously. Ronnie always put me on an undeserving pedestal after that, and that was all she wrote. We were best buds, joined at the hip, even though I was mischief, incarnate.

I was a holy terror from the start. Mother blamed it on a tornado that almost blew our house away one night, when I was only a few months old. She said as the storm passed over the house, it looked like the walls were breathing, but that I never cried a tear. She believed it was some kind of sign. I don't know about signs, but I do know that life has always been an interesting roller coaster ride since then. I am a peaceful girl, but don't try to push me into a corner or I come out fighting like a wildcat. Or else I catch you quietly when you are least expecting it.

When I was three, we moved to the big city of Tupelo (actually a tiny town then, but it was prospering). This, was 1956, when a young Tupelo native named Elvis Presley was making headlines. Elvis had come home to sing at a concert at the fairgrounds. It is now legendary, but I was too little to remember that day. I saw plenty of pictures later in life, but Ronnie who was seven years older than I, did get to hear it all, and was transformed. This was the beginning of a magical time that lasted for most of our childhood years.

We were dirt poor, as they called it, but we were rich in friends, family, love and faith. We had a small frame house on Lumpkin Street in Tupelo, and there was always someone there. My Mother was divorced, scandalous for that time period, but she was a tough lady, and had plenty of reason for getting single. My grandparents also lived with us, as my grandfather, who was an excellent barber, had fallen on ill health. He could only work part time, as his leg, which had been badly burned in an auto accident, would not allow him to stand for long periods at a time. Doctors had told him he would never be able to walk again, due to the severity of that injury, but that's the kind of grit, determination and stubbornness that is our family.

Many of these stories (memories) reflect daily adventures in our lives that made us laugh and sometimes cry. Life unplugged.

Never take your stories for granted, no matter how big or small they may be. Savor them like fine wine and pass them on with love.

Don't Blow Up the Backyard

When The Preacher is Visiting

Long ago and far away in another lifetime, there were mischievous boys. Not mean or venomous boys, just mischievous, extremely intelligent, and bored out of their minds during the end of summer boys. If an "idle mind is the devil's workshop", well it might have started here.

Summer had trailed into a beautiful autumn and the beginning of a new school year. After a long and eventful summer, everyone was still adjusting to the new routine of classes and homework and not as much free time. How ever it was currently the weekend. Free time was theirs for the taking.

As I have explained previously, in another story it came to be that the boys had learned at the local library over the summer, how to make gunpowder! Now in today's world this would have been a real problem as times have changed greatly since the early sixties. In fact, it hardly resembles the free, imaginative world that I grew up in. Many times, I long for those simpler days and the chance to be a creative, imaginative child without being thought of as a menace to society. I am certain that we did some things we probably shouldn't have done, but in this time period, parents ruled with discipline, a good belt and the fear of God! And there was the 'talking to" tongue lashing that was far worse than any spanking or grounding. Things were different then but it mostly worked.

So, the boys had made many different batches of gunpowder by now. They tried various experiments

like trying to make fireworks and blowing up plastic soldiers, the ones they hadn't already melted with a good sun ray and a magnifying glass. Just blowing holes in the ground and exploding things in drainage culverts was also interesting. After all culverts had that great echo. And most everything was tried just out of ear shot of home or parents. As the smaller explosions became rather boring, things escalated a bit. One might see where this is heading. It was destined to happen sooner or later, but it turned out to be a lot sooner than later.

It was a bright, clear blue, cloudless Sunday afternoon in early Autumn. Leaves had begun their slow swirling dance with mother nature, but the temperature was still just warm enough to be delightful. The air was dry and there was a slight southerly breeze today. Church was over a couple hours ago, and it was the perfect afternoon. At home, grandma had served a Sunday dinner fit for a king, but in this case, it was for the preacher. She had her amazing fried chicken, mashed potatoes, beans and cornbread, sweet tea and two desserts. The kids had been fed early and sent to the yard to play so the grownups could talk and we were meant to be on our best behavior.

That statement became short lived, as one of the boys quietly asked my brother Ronnie, "Wonder what would happen if we put some powder in that old pipe?" They had a quick debate and determined that probably nothing would happen and that it would probably fizzle out, make minimal noise and not cause any real damage. Teenage curiosity got the better of them and they packed it up tight and buried it and stuck a fuse in it. None of them thought it would do anything, but they got very surprised, because essentially folks this was a pipe bomb!

The pipe had come as a leftover remnant of a plumber's recent visit. I don't know what all they did in stuffing the pipe that day, as gunpowder wasn't my forte until much later.

After they had buried it, I got closer to the house, because in my head, I was thinking that this might be a really bad idea, but the deed was on.

As always, the skinny kid had to light the fuse because he could run faster. And so, he did, and then the countdown, five, four, three, two... it didn't get to one, KABOOOOOMMMM!!!

"Holy crap" I yelled. The sound was deafening and windows rattled in their frames. The house shook. A heavy push of air rushed hard across the yard almost toppling the kids. Debris went flying everywhere. We all looked at each other for a brief second and then came my mother flying out the back door! Grandma, grandpa, the preacher, neighbors, visiting aunts and uncles and even the dogs! It was a sight to behold! Mother thought at first the water heater had exploded, but then she knew in an instant! She then exploded all over us and made more noise than the gunpowder. She looked around first to make sure no body parts were missing and then she yelled for everybody to “leave now” and she yelled after the boys, "Just wait until your mothers hear this one". Then

Ronnie and I were summoned into the house with mother's single sharp but quiet "Now".

It was not a pretty sight after the preacher left. I think she broke a beaded Indian belt on Ronnie's behind, simply because of the adrenaline from being so scared. I skated off scot-free with no problem as I was simply an innocent bystander. Right. But it worked to my advantage. There was grounding and grounding and more grounding. Ronnie kept trying to make her understand that they only did it out of curiosity to see what would happen (like the time he put his hand in an iron grate to see if his hand would fit... it didn't, it went in, but it wouldn't come out), and there was the sulfur smoke bomb he made that mother was allergic to, and many more adventures). But in the end, there was only so much yelling she could do. We were sent to our rooms as tomorrow was a school day and for once, school seemed a blessing.

Things quieted down in a few days and neighbors started speaking again, and soon the autumn days turned cooler and thoughts turned to Halloween. Thoughts and comments about the pipe bomb vanished with dreams of goblins, and parties and candy.

But the pipe bomb adventure seared into the deepest parts of my brain along with a smile, and a sweet memory to hide in the folds of my heart. I will never forget those glorious days of total freedom and my love of my childhood friends.

I can still see the explosion after all these years and every time I do, I smile, and not just a little smile, but I smile like a cheshire cat. And wherever all the boys have come to be, I still love each and every one of you, pinky swear

The Untimely Death of the Radio Antenna

Sometime around the time that I was in the first or second grade, my brother, Ronnie inherited an old round-top, antique, radio from his Uncle Billy. Now, Uncle Billy was quite a character and lived to be 101 years old. This was after he had been told as a young man that he had six months to live. So, Billy enjoyed every minute of his life, from those six months to the ripe old age of101 years.

In those days, the early sixties, an old radio was still a treasure for any kid. Television was relatively new, and shows were still in black and white. Most shows were westerns or game shows. Everyone was fascinated by tv, but they were quite expensive to own and many folks still relied on radios for home entertainment. And they still loved their radios.

Although radio programming was mostly music now, it was still dotted with old time radio shows, and all the kids loved radios too. Transistor radios, pocket sized portable radios, were just coming into existence and with a simple battery, one could be entertained for hours. However, these new portables were also expensive items at the time.

Ronnie tried hooking up his prized radio in the house, but the signal was mostly static. He needed a bigger and better antenna for a stronger signal. But instead of asking any grownups for help or advice, he and his friends hatched a plan to put up an antenna outside that would be attached and tethered to the house, like the new tv antennas. This particular group of friends had almost become notorious for their antics lately, and had no doubt they could get the job done. The guys decided if a big antenna was good for a tv it must be an excellent choice for a radio!

I'm not quite sure where the antenna came from, but a couple of days later, there it was laying in our backyard. The guys were always dragging something to our house that someone had given them or they had traded for. Sometimes they would do odd jobs or mow lawns, but they usually got what they wanted. Keeping in mind we were all just kids and experience was how you learned things.

The time came for the install. I don't know why the grownups didn't notice, but it was on. While the guys struggled to wrangle the antenna against the side of the house, they sent me inside to get some tools, hammer, nails, wire, whatever. They didn't plan very well is all I know. I was bad about getting distracted anyway, but when I went inside, my grandmother, had made me a tomato sandwich. As this was one of my favorite things, I took a few minutes to sit down and eat it. I had almost forgotten my outside mission, but suddenly I felt the urge to go and said to myself, "I'm really going get yelled at." So off I went to get things. I don't know how long I was in the house, or what exactly happened. But as I headed out the door something was happening and it wasn't good!
As if in slow motion, the antenna was falling away from the house. I think it had to be fifteen or twenty feet tall, at least that's what it looked like to a six-year-old kid. It continued to fall, but it didn't land in our yard, oh no. It landed, full up and hooked, over the power lines that went across the width of the backyard. Several boys were still struggling to hold it up. Fortunately, most of them were knocked off the pole and were scattered all over the back yard. But James Alvin was stuck to the pole like molasses with electricity zapping his body. Ronnie, remembered some Boy Scout training, grabbed a wooden 2x4 that was laying in the yard and knocked him off the pole. It's a wonder the 2x4 didn't break his ribs, but it worked and James

scrambled away like a squirrel. But all that electricity was still putting on a cosmic show and all the insulation was melting and dripping off the lines into the yard. Power had now gone out for two blocks and neighbors began popping out of their houses.

In due time, the power company arrived and had to retrieve the antenna off the line. Mom was just getting home from work on the bus. I just remember her screaming to the top of her lungs and then hugging everyone she could get her hands on. At this time the antenna had still been on the power lines doing its sizzle and pop.

The next day, we made the newspaper. No names were mentioned but there was a story about a power outage in West Tupelo that covered over two blocks. And just a note, the power company had to install brand new power lines across three yards!

Mom said Ronnie was grounded for life. She actually said that a lot, but she surely did hug him a lot that week. Guess maybe I should have passed up that tomato sandwich, but they still have a powerful control over me. The radio never did get a real antenna but it sat in the house for years and years on a high shelf. But Ronnie and his friends went on to even greater adventures.

The Boys and the Chemistry Set

In another lifetime, when television was brand new and microwaves were years from invention. Back before Homeland Security, terrorists, political correctness, or the internet. Before folks trying to save you from yourself or folks minding all your business, there were simpler times. In the era of the late fifties and early sixties there were very intelligent. but very bored kids.

In my tiny rural town, down South, there was a small group of boys, my brother included, who were notorious with their mischievous natures, and getting into trouble from their exuberant curiosity. Or as some called it, creative mischief.

Back in this time period kids usually got really cool presents on birthdays and at Christmas, but not so much the rest of the year, as money was always a bit scarce. Gifts for boys were usually science or sports related. And although sports gifts were king, a new science interest was raging, due in part to the new space race. Hopefully little boys would grow up to be scientists or astronauts who would magically save the world, or fly off into space. As yet, they had no idea what a whirlwind girls would later make.

That being said, a most popular gift for boys, was a chemistry set. There were multiple types of sets and it got quite interesting when the boys learned how to share and trade their contents. These 'toys' were not, watered down. They contained enough articles, weather instruments, microscopes, measuring devices, gyro scopes, and lots of real chemicals for mixing some major experiments. Most came in large metal fold out cases with places to store these treasures for future use.

And then, there was the public library. Since the internet was years from being born, the library was the greatest source of information to be found. The boys spent a great deal of time at the library. One of their quests became, how to make gun powder. The search for how to make gunpowder came as a result of the question, how do cowboys get the gunpowder in their bullets? And, they figured it all out, including making the stuff. They were able to buy what extra ingredients they needed at a pharmacy, to go with what they had in the chemistry sets and yes, they made gun powder! Soon, they were playing and experimenting, trying to make fireworks and such, but then they got a crazier idea. And parents did not have a clue.

Around Halloween, one of the kids got the idea, and double dog dared the others, to put gun powder in one of the cannons at the Civil War memorial on West Main Street. And that was that. A double dog dare meant it was on.

It was night time, a few days before Halloween and they did put gun powder in one of the cannons and stuffed it with bodock apples (the big green, milky, hairy grapefruit sized fruit of the southern bodock tree). The skinniest kid, James was left to light the fuse, as he could always run the fastest. The others waited patiently across the highway. Then a flash and KABOOM!

Pieces of bodock apples splattered everywhere! The night air shattered with the noise, but windows of nearby houses, shook in their frames. The caretaker of the memorial, who lived across the street, was out his door in a flash, and was seen running out in his underwear, but the boys were long gone.

In the morning, the boys feared they were going to die, but it was eerily quiet. The explosion didn't even make the newspaper and the kids breathed a sigh of relief vowing to never do anything that crazy again. But that was short lived. Until another time, when the preacher was visiting one Sunday afternoon. But that is a tale for another day.

The big chemistry set my brother had is long gone, as is my brother, but he and all those precious boys will live in my heart forever.

Afternoon Dumpster Diving

In the days before fancy daycares there were parents finding creative ways to take care of their kids. My mom was one such person and since she worked five and a half days a week and was a single parent in the late fifties and early sixties, she had to be very creative. Her challenge was to take care of two kids, spaced seven years apart and her aging parents. There is no amount of saying “I’m sorry” that can ever make up for all the things we did, but she did an awesome job. I just wish I could be half the person she was.

On Saturday afternoons when she finally got off work, my brother and I would ride the city bus to go meet her downtown. That might sound big, but Tupelo, was a very small town. We were just lucky enough to have a basic public transportation system in place. Although the town pretty much ran three old privately owned school buses for its system, it still got the job done and many people were just glad to have a way to get around a fairly rural community.

Each Saturday my mom, my brother Ronnie, and I would run errands, go shopping and buy groceries and then catch the last bus home. Everything was downtown. For those who haven't lived it, there was no mall, no shopping centers, no cell phones, no texting, no video games, no microwaves and few people had cars. Though you would think it primitive today, it was wonderful! We had to create our own entertainment for the most part, although there were two movie theaters downtown.

There were drug stores downtown, a bakery, a post office, places to shop for clothes, shoe stores, hardware stores, banks, places to buy appliances, furniture stores, jewelry stores, grocery stores, hotels, churches, a Woolworth's, and the local newspaper. And awesome places like Ben Franklin's Five and Dime store called dime stores. Of course, you used to be able to buy a lot with a dime. This layout was quite a variety for a small town like Tupelo, and all this business and pleasure was incorporated into about nine to twelve blocks.

And also, prepare to be shocked, there were no fast-food places on every corner! We had a couple of diners, but I can only think of one real restaurant. The one I remember had a huge plastic bull on top of the building in later years, and that bull usually ended up on top of the local high school each year close to graduation time. There was however, TKE and T&S Drug stores. And both had lunch counters with excellent food.

TKE Drugs had a larger lunch counter. And they had the best, juicy hot dogs imaginable. We would go every Saturday for hot dogs and potato salad and a Coke. Honestly, I can still smell that delightful aroma. This place was a kid's dream. Not only did we get our school workbooks and supplies here in the fall, they had comic books! We would slide down the lunch counter stools and go sit on the edge of the comic book stands and read until someone ran us off or it was time to go home.

On weekdays after school when we had reached the junior high level, we would walk from school sometimes to downtown to meet mom at her work and ride home with her on the bus. Since my brother was a good bit older, he and his after-school friends found a variety of other creative entertainment, which did not always sit well with my mom. Of course, some days, most days actually, the boys rode their bikes and mostly kept to themselves. I didn't have a bike, so I walked.

One particular afternoon, Ronnie and his friends rode their usual trek downtown, but ended up cutting through the alleys behind some of the businesses and were attracted, as kids will be, to piles of garbage waiting to be picked up by the garbage folks. A boy cannot let an opportunity like this pass him by and soon they were all "dumpster diving". There were tons of old office supplies that were at one time useful, but had been tossed out for unknown reasons. There were bundles of old, unused paper, folders, receipts and old envelopes with paper bands still around them holding them together in bundles. A virtual wonderland for kids.

The boys picked out several discarded treasures, and then proceeded to pile up bunches of the old paper, pads and envelopes on their bicycles, and took off down the street. I'm not quite sure what happened, but it was a blustery day and the old bands around the stacks of paper and envelopes decided at that moment that they had stuck together for as long as they were going to in this world. As the boys were crossing Main Street, a big gust of wind sucked all that paper up into a huge swirling cloud. It was suddenly a huge dust-devil paper storm and went flying all over a half block or more down Main Street. Then all of a sudden, the wind stopped just as abruptly as it had started, and dusty old paper literally rained down from the sky for what seemed like an eternity and went sailing everywhere! It flew down sidewalks full of people, over their heads, bounced into buildings and went swirling all over and under traffic, landing on windshields and setting off the shrill shriek of automobiles braking. It was a site for a kid to behold and be momentarily in awe.

Unfortunately for Ronnie, my mother heard about it almost immediately, as she got a phone call asking her did, she know where her son was that afternoon. It seems some of our neighbors had been in one of those cars dodging paper. She was hopping mad at the embarrassment, and soon had my brother out picking up every scrap of paper for quite a few blocks.

I don't think Ronnie ever decided to dumpster dive again. If he did, he kept it to himself or only told his friends. I surely do miss my big brother. He was one of a kind.

Earl

Ronald Earl Gentry was my grandfather. He was born in the summer of 1893.and was the son of James R, Gentry and Rena Belle Harper. Rena was a housewife and James was a schoolteacher, an admirable profession in the 1800's, but they also farmed. The family lived around Baldwyn, Mississippi for many decades.

Earl met the love of his life when he was five years old at church. He said that he thought she was the most beautiful thing he had ever seen with her jet-black hair and beautiful brown eyes. She was part French. Her name was Ildra (ILDRA)Mullennix. Her Father descended from the French family, Molineux, but his parents changed the spelling of their name when they came to America. William Molineux/Mullennix, died quite young, leaving several small children, one of which was Ildra. Earl's parents never had any trouble getting him to go to church after that meeting. She loved him, as much as he loved her and that note always rang true. They were eventually married one beautiful day in the back of a wagon.

Earl's parents died young too, and as he was the oldest male in the family, he and Ildra assumed the responsibility of raising all five siblings. He had many dreams he had to let go of to support the children. They farmed to stay afloat, but as the young ones got old enough to be out on their own, Earl decided to take barber training and become a barber. This was a very noble profession, as in those times barbers did much more than cut hair. Eventually, Earl was soon recognized at his profession and was soon asked to teach others, which he was happy to do. One of the tests he gave his students was to shave a balloon with a straight razor.

Years later, after he and Ildra had raised their daughter Christine, he worked in shops all over Mississippi. As I was growing up, he used to tell me all kinds of tales and adventures he had during his life. I would sit for hours just to listen to him spin stories, many from barber shops.

One such story he used to tell was when he worked in a barber shop in downtown New Albany, Mississippi. There was an older man that used to come into his shop every Saturday. He said you could set a clock by his routines, and he was known to be quite frugal. But my grand-father loved everyone, so their quirks and such never bothered him in the least. One particular Saturday the man came in to get a haircut and a shave and when it was his turn, he climbed into the barber chair as normal. Grandpa went about his business, but as the man was sitting there, he crossed his legs in the chair. Earl just happened to look up at that moment and noticed there was something wrong with the man's feet. They didn't look right. He tried not to stare or cause him any embarrassment, but something was off, and momentarily he couldn't figure out what it was. As he finished up the shave, the man started to get up and uncrossed his legs. Then his feet were supposed to look normal, but they still didn't! Then it hit Earl, this man was wearing his shoes on the wrong feet! As he had never seen this before, he blurted out before thinking "Do you realize that you have your shoes on the wrong feet?"

"Oh sure, Earl" the man replied. I wear them like this every other week to even the heels out. Saves me money on getting them repaired." Grandpa just shook his head as the man walked out the door; his shoes still on backwards.

Another Saturday, my brother's dog tore the pants off another customer in the barber shop. But we'll get into that later.

Surely wish I could hear him spin me a story today and I hope he's at the gate when I get to heaven. Love you, Daddy Earl!

The Funeral

Warning if you are sensitive about funerals, you might want to find a different story to read. This was my first memory that dug into my young head and not all memories are pleasant, but hopefully they are sometimes beneficial to others.

Many people debate on whether a young child should be allowed to go to a funeral. While everything in life has a time and place, I believe it depends on the situation. When I was a small child, I did not have a choice in the matter and this particular memory is ingrained in my soul forever. If the events had not played out as they did, it probably would have just been a small memory, jumbled in with all the millions of others floating around in my head.

It was August and I was five, Actually, I had only been five for several months. My great grandfather had died and although it was my great grandmother's second husband, it was tragic. The funeral was to be held in a small town up the road about an hour or so away. My mother worked during the week so my grandmother took care of me and this day, she needed to be at the funeral, so it was decided that I would go with her. This would be my first experience with funerals. My family did not have a car, so we got a ride with my grandmother's sister and her husband.

So off we went, the four of us to the funeral. It had been raining all week and had been raining this morning as well, but fortunately it had stopped for now and the sun was trying to peek through the gray, low hanging clouds.

We arrived at the church a little early. Several folks had already arrived and the casket had just been brought into the church. In those years, funeral parlors, as they were called then, were not widely available, or used much when they were available, as the idea was, they were quite impersonal. In the South there was a long tradition, whereby family members or other close relatives would have the deceased person's body in a casket in the person's home overnight. Visitation as we know it today, would be at the home, and friends and relatives would visit there and bring food and condolences. Someone would sit up with the body all night, called sitting with the dead, until the following day of the funeral, so the deceased would not be alone. The next day just before the funeral, the body would be taken to the church the deceased had attended.

The ceremony at the church began. Everything proceeded as normal until the service was almost over. It then began to rain again. Not just a little rain, but a full-on storm with hard, frequent streaks of lightning and booming thunder, shaking the walls of the tiny wooden church.

I had gotten as close as was possible to grandmother and I could feel the nervous tension in her as she held me by the shoulders and told me everything would be okay.

As the service ended there was confusion as to what to do about the burial. Folks waited around for about an hour for the storm to end, and finally it slowed to a light trickle. Outside water was standing in the low parking lot and trickling down the hill to lower spots. This had essentially been a cloud burst and a small flood, but tiny streaks of sunlight began to momentarily shoot long triangles of light through the lingering clouds.

Everyone that was left at the church by this time got in their cars and headed to the cemetery. My great uncle parked just outside the gate as we rolled up to the cemetery, as he thought the women should just stay in the car. It was only about fifty feet to the gravesite, but we did as he asked and stayed in the car. At this distance

however, everything was still in plain sight of where we were sitting.
The preacher finished the graveside service and the pall bearers began to put the casket in the ground. Remember there is no funeral home staff to help, so the pall bearers and other men, if needed, would lower the casket into the ground and fill in the grave. The problem was that it had rained, so much, that the red clay hole they needed to put the casket in was full of water. At first, they got buckets and tried to bail the water out of the hole, but they soon realized, that there was too much water and that bailing wasn't working very well. So, they put the casket on top of the hole, floating it on the water and began to try to sink it down to the bottom. I watched, transfixed. I couldn't take my eyes off that sight. My grandmother was also noticeably upset. She murmured what are they doing? By now one man, and then several others actually got on top of the casket trying to force it into the hole. As water began to run out of the sides of the hole, more men climbed on top, until the casket was covered, as if by monsters, but then, it finally began to sink. Water was now spewing out the sides and covered the top as it went into the ground. All the men were soaking wet in their floppy suits. Then they started trying to shovel mud on top. I remember I started crying. It was just one of those things that should never happen. It had looked like a dozen men on top. I just remember it was like a

horror movie. They finally got everything settled and when my uncle came back to the car, he was wet, muddy and visibly shaken.
Everyone was very quiet as he started the car and we began to move.

I'm not sure what happened next, but the car slid off the road into a very deep ditch, that was also full of water and I got slammed against the door. I remember screaming, as I thought I was going to be swept away by the water. We ended up crawling out the other side into the road. Someone went home and got a tractor to pull the car out and it began to rain hard again.

A group of those same men who had been on top of the casket were the ones who got us out of the ditch. I dreamed about this day for several weeks, that they were coming for me. Unfortunately, it was one of the first vivid memories I had of my childhood, but I survived the day. I can still see it in my mind though, just like a polaroid snapshot.

So, be careful what you expose young children too. It can leave a forever mark. I have recalled this event many times over the years, and I hope no one ever experiences something like this, but times and funerals are different now and I hope it stays that way.

Halloween Magic

Halloween, except for Christmas is the all-time favorite of kids. Getting to carve spooky pumpkins and put candles in them was a delight. Having pumpkin contests at school, and thinking about candy for a month before was good for day dreaming. What kid didn't love being turned loose by parents to roam the streets with the largest bag, plastic pumpkin, or garbage bag one could find, and to come home with said accessory filled to the brim with luscious treats and candies? Sugar highs duly noted.

The 'loot' had the potential to last for days, so planning the route to get to all the best stuff was a must. Also, planning costumes was imperative. You couldn't have two ghosts show up at a door. That would be unfashionable and was unacceptable! "What are you going to be this year"? "Dunno, what are you going to be"? This dialogue could go on for days or weeks, but something always materialized like magic. And in the end all types of interesting ideas were born from clowns and witches to Superman and Wonder Woman, along with princesses, cowboys, Indians, ship captains, Lone Rangers, pirates, ghosts, Roy Rogers and Dale Evans, Cisco Kids, vampires, mummies, doctors, nurses, Frankenstein and all types of monsters and every other type of ghoul, zombie or dead looking character a kid could imagine. Halloween 'was' imagination, something that is sorely lacking in the world today.

The night air in late October would have just begun to cool from the hot, steamy summers we experience in the South. Fostering dreams of falling leaves, homework, football games and of course, Thanksgiving and Christmas, but first comes Halloween.

The appointed time would finally arrive. It seemed like forever before the sun began to set and we bolted off like race horses out of a shoot to experience our heart thumping adventures. Our first stop was to take care of the trick-or-treating at hand.

For the inexperienced, prime time candy 'scarfing' consisted of anything chocolate. Dark chocolate, light chocolate, milk chocolate, white chocolate, chocolate with peanuts, chocolate with almonds or cocoanut, who cares? It was chocolate! Chocolate was king. The goal of the evening was to rake it in.

Before the days of mean people 'dosing' kids candy treats, one might find almost anything in a treat bag. There might be apples, oranges, candy apples, popcorn balls, muffins, rice crispy treats, or even money! Actually, any treat that was thrown in the bag was good. If you didn't like something you could trade it. It was 'loot' to savor for days to come and it was ours!

Spotted around the area were other forms of Halloween adventure. There were haunted houses (usually in a family's garage) that had been created to give the kids an extra scare. We were usually blindfolded and led through the maze of spaghetti brains, fake spider webs, grape eyeballs, and hot dog fingers in cooled syrup filled trays along with creepy moans and groans and mood music, usually of distant screams. Some adults were better at putting these horror houses together than others, but being blindfolded really helped the imagination experience.

And there were the Halloween carnivals, festivals, parties and wonderful hayrides. The carnivals had all sorts of kid games. All fixed so the little ones could win small prizes to add to their trick –or-treat loot. Bobbing for apples was always a favorite as it was an excuse to get soaked to the bone and not get yelled at for doing so. For moms and dads, someone invented the cake walk, which in Southern Bible belt regions was considered 'gambling' and since they considered Halloween a pagan ritual, eventually led to the demise of carnivals for years. Later on, carnivals were changed to 'fall or Harvest Festivals' and for some reason this made it okay again. I don't pretend to understand the musings of the adult mind, as, personally, I never plan to grow up.

Hayrides were the best event going. One usually had to be invited to one of these events though, so they were extra special. Lots of spooky zombies and such were out in the pastures trailing the open-bed trailer. Who knew zombies, mummies and werewolves lived on the family farm? Some folks will remember their first kiss on a hayride too. Hayrides were good for all kinds of stories for retelling.

Of course there were other kids, mostly older, who were determined to stir up mischief. They egged houses and people, soaped windows, rolled yards with toilet paper and one year I saw a yard someone had covered by sticking individual plastic forks all over the yard! Now that took some patience. I decided most of these kids were just jealous because they were getting too big to trick-or-treat.

The last stop of my troop's Halloween evening would always be the witch's house! She was a Halloween staple in our neighborhood. She was an older lady who lived on the corner close to my house and always went out of her way to see we had a special evening. She was always in full witch attire from her big pointed hat, long black hair, and pasty-white face, to her pointed black shoes. Her decorated broom stood by the door waiting for her next ride and in the yard, she had an enormous black kettle that a couple of children would fit in nicely. That kettle was always fogging, but from dry ice, not a fire. Inside the kettle were ice cold sodas and all manner of drinks for thirsty trick-or-treaters who were out late and trying to drag home their huge sacks of candy.

The witch-lady kept up with you all year. She had a huge book that you had to sign when you visited her house. After signing the book, you were allowed to enter her spooky kitchen by the back door. That kitchen trumped any of the haunted houses. She had all that and more, and even had shrunken heads. But her kitchen table always out-weighed anyone being scared. She had all the usual candy treats, but she had apples, oranges, and bananas, rice crispy treats, popcorn balls, chocolate cake, coconut cake, pumpkin pie, muffins, little loaves of homemade bread and more. And unlike other places, you could haul off all you wanted, within reason. Funny thing, kids usually just took what was fair. She was such an amazing lady and you didn't want a witch mad at you anyways.

At other times of the year, the witch had the best apple trees ever, in her backyard. I know those apples had a spell on them as I have never seen one so red, or tasted one as sweet and juicy as the ones we would sneak from those trees. She had heavy log chains hanging all in the trees. She said something about something in the chains nurturing them.

So, Halloween became one of my favorite holidays and still is. I wish I could go back to the witch's house just one more time on a crisp fall evening when electricity and magic filled the air. Some of the best memories of my life go back to Halloween, and those glorious evenings we roamed so free.

Forgotten

Tupelo, Mississippi has always been an interesting place, but in the late fifties and through-out the sixties it was an amazing small town and a wonderful place for kids to grow up. As there was little crime in those days (yes, there was crime, but not like today), kids were free to roam to their heart's content (for most part) to their own discretion. When streetlights came on at dark, it was a signal to be inside the house and washing up for dinner. This was a good thing. Children knew the unwritten rules and kept to those rules as the idea of daycare had not even been created yet.

There were various activities and organizations to help keep the small folk occupied and in check such as Boy Scouts, Girl Scouts, church programs such as Girls Auxiliary, (GA's) Royal Ambassadors

(RA's), choir practice, and of course the main sports of football, basketball and baseball.

So, as I had become the ripe old age of eleven, I had entered Junior High School at the local middle school called Milam. This had given me the privilege of becoming a free agent of sorts to roam at will (well almost) at least until I had to meet my mom everyday downtown to go home with her. Mom worked at the Tupelo Daily Journal as an accountant. During this time period the newspaper was located on Magazine Street until they moved to their current location on Green Street.

I had several options every day after school until five o'clock. I could stop off at the library which I loved to do or I could go to a movie at the little Tupelo Theater on Main Street, across from Kermit's Bakery. I saw many an Agatha Christie movie there. Another option if I had some change was to go to Woolworth's and sit at the lunch counter and have a soda or some lemonade. Or I could even venture down Spring Street and go to the Ben Franklin Five and Dime store. Mostly I just liked to dream and window shop. At any rate, five p.m. would always come around and I knew to be at her office or in front of Woolworth's.

One afternoon, mom had told me to meet her at Woolworth's as soon as I could walk to town after school. She said she was getting off early and we would go shopping before we went home. She said to go straight there and wait for her. So, after school I went straight there and went to the lunch counter to get a drink while I waited. By three forty-five she hadn't come, but I figured she was just running late. I got up and started looking at things all over the store to pass the time. It was about four twenty by now and I was getting fidgety. Where could she be?

During this time the store was playing music overhead, but they kept playing the same song over and over. It was of all things, Johnny Cash singing 'Ring of Fire'. Well after I listened to Johnny about fifty times singing "I went down, down, down and the flames went higher", I began to panic. It was now five p.m. and still no mom.

I was just about to ask a store employee if I could use their phone. I had spent all my change on my drink and didn't have money for the pay phone. About that time, I saw her. Mom came flying in the door and I went running to her. She went down on one knee and hugged me. Then I was terrified because I thought something horrible had happened and started crying my heart out. She just said "Baby, I am so sorry, I forgot you!" Then I cried even harder. I soon realized it had hurt her more than it had hurt me. She had made it all the way home and had almost missed the last bus to get home. She had a horrible day and actually got off work later than usual. As soon as she got there, she remembered me and was horrified. She had to get a taxi to take her all the way back to town to find me, just as the store was about to close. And believe me this was a luxury we could not afford, but it was an emergency. She kept her arm around me all the way home.

My grandmother, who lived with us, told me later she had burst out crying when she realized she had left me. Poor Mom.

I don't know how she raised me and my brother as a single parent and also took care of her two aging parents who were living with us. I knew even then how much she sacrificed for us and I never forgot that love. I wish I could feel the safety of her arms wrap around me one more time.

And just a note. Every once in a while, when I am really tired or quiet and letting my mind wander, I sometimes hear a voice in my head singing,

"And it burns, burns, burns
that ring of fire,
that ring of fire".

Yes, I know, I remember every word to this day.

Washing Dishes is Good for the Soul

I'll admit that from time to time I am a mischievous scoundrel. Nothing really mean, just little things that can grab someone's attention, usually when they need a lesson in manners and such. Most folks tend to think I am absolutely predictable, but they would be folks that don't quite know me. I do have my moments. You have to learn something when neighbor kids stick dead frogs to your door, but that's a story for another day.

Years back, my brother Ronnie and I had found ourselves left to our own devices to live, so we were living in a small house in the neighborhood we grew up in. Friends, acquaintances, neighbors and such were always dropping by. I'm not quite sure what the fascination was, but we loved them all. We watched a lot of tv, movies had deep conversations, cooked a lot when we had money and loved to stay up late. We were total night owls.

While as previously stated I always loved most everyone who dropped by, but there were a couple of people that came to be what my grandmother would term, "proverbial pests". This was the type of person who would never say anything good about anyone, always took the negative approach to everything, was full of drama and never helped a lick when it came to helping folks. But this one decided to become a permanent dinner guest!

It was so strange. He always showed up at our house at dinner time. Don't misunderstand here. We both loved to have folks come over to eat, but the truth was we were young and not making a lot of money at the time. We couldn't afford to feed someone every day that never helped out a bit. No matter what time I fixed food it was like a dinner bell rang somewhere and he could hear it. And it wasn't like he was broke. He always had plenty of money for any other thing that crossed his fancy.

Anyway. One night I hatched a plan. If any of you have read many of my other stories, you know that I had a black, fuzzy part Labrador puppy named Uppie. The family we got her from had a little girl that couldn't yet say puppy, so she called them "uppies". So, we called our puppy, Uppie. Uppie was quite a dog. He would open the bottom cabinet door, where we stored his food. When he got hungry, he would get himself a can of dog food and drop it at your feet! And sometimes it was if he could read my mind.

On one particular night I didn't have much money in the budget for food. Fortunately, I had enough stored up in the pantry to throw together a small dinner of beef stroganoff, salad and bread. I also had ingredients to make a pie. So, I pulled that one out of the hat. But sure enough, I had just called my brother to the table, and in walks the company! Sometimes, like now, he would just stroll in the door if you forgot to lock it. I was my usual hostess self as my mother had taught me to always be gracious, whatever the situation. So, I went to get another plate and a drink, but by the time I walked back to the table he was sitting in my chair at my plate and slurping away. As I sat down, he was going for seconds. Fortunately, Ronnie had got his first, but all I had left was scraps and a few bites of salad. Usually, I really wouldn't care, but I was tired and hungry. I was pretty ticked off. They were still sitting at the table as I started clearing the dishes. Of course, I still had the cleanup to go.

I walked over to the sink with the rest of the dishes but instead of running water, I called my four-legged helper over. With company in perfect view,

Uppie and I began washing dishes. I put a plate in the floor and he licked it clean. I sat that one in the dish drainer and set another one in the floor. We did every dish, glass, pot and pan. I thought I caught a strange look out of the corner of my eye, but we kept moving ahead, and soon we were done. No one said a word. Ronnie had figured me out as usual and was about to burst out laughing, but he stayed quiet.
"Anybody want some pie" I said? Funny, I didn't have any takers at the moment. I got myself a clean plate and dug in. When I got alone, I laughed until I nearly cried. And of course, I went back after he left and thoroughly washed my dishes.

And the next night? For the first time in ages, he didn't show up at dinner. Oh, he still came around to lounge, but funny thing he brought himself some take out.

And Uppie? He got lots of hugs and I thought I saw him wink at me; he and I had a ball washing our dishes. We found out laughter, lots of mischief and washing dishes, was good for the soul.

Turkey Day to Remember

Holidays. Some people love them, some people hate them, but with holidays, comes all that wonderful food and loved ones. All the years I spent at home, we always had a feast, and every relative and friend we had always ended up at our house. Magical memories and amazing food, shared by all.

After my grandmother passed away and my mom remarried the love of her life and moved away to California, my brother and I found ourselves on our own as Thanksgiving was approaching. It appeared we would be fending for ourselves this year but closer to the big day, we found that we had three dinner invitations from which to choose. After a little thought, I quickly thanked everyone for the invitations, but told them that I wanted to attempt to cook my first Thanksgiving dinner this year!

A couple of days before the occasion, I collected tried and true recipes from friends and relatives and went grocery shopping. I got all the traditional goodies including a small turkey. I was so excited. The day came. And I actually got up early to get a head start on everything.I got out my recipe collection and soon had my moms' chicken and dressing cooking while I whipped up a green bean casserole and put the potatoes on to cook. The turkey was now roasting in a slow oven and getting basted occasionally with white wine. I also put on some corn and made deviled eggs. The smell was heavenly!

My neighbor Lucille, a sweet little lady that lived across the street, called to tell me she had baked me two pies. She laughed and said she wanted to contribute to Thanksgiving history as she knew this was my first holiday cooking by myself. Looking back, this was almost prophetic considering later events. I thanked her and told her I would be over as soon as my turkey was out of the oven.

It was getting pretty warm and stuffy in the kitchen by now, so I raised the glass panel on the storm door to let in the nice cool breeze.

Soon the potatoes were done, mashed and set aside on the counter. All the other food was done and set aside on the counter too. I just needed to open the cranberry sauce and make tea. The turkey, now crisp and brown, was ready to come out of the oven. I had run out of counter space to put things though so I just put the pan on the table on some towels to rest before it got carved.

Time to go get my pies I thought. I believed this would only take a few minutes. It turned out to be more than a few minutes, but the pies were beautiful. She had made me a chocolate and a pecan and I had some ice cream at home. I thanked her, hugged her and started back across the street. I needed to get the table set as my brother, Ronnie had gone to pick up his two friends, and they were on the way.

As I came in the front door I heard a strange loud noise. It was a banging noise like something beating on metal and it was coming from the kitchen! What in the world? I panicked as I thought something might be about to explode. I sat the pies down in the living room and hurried to the kitchen. As I rounded the corner, I saw what had made the banging sound. It was the sound of my roasting pan beating up and down on the kitchen floor. It took a moment to register the large dog with the turkey in his mouth, but there it was. I think I screamed to the top of my lungs. I do know that's when the sailor swearing started. Words came out of my mouth that I didn't even know I knew.

Thump, thump, thump; with every thump, another bite was gone! Uppie, my black, fuzzy part Labrador dog was standing by the table, paws deep in the roasting pan devouring Thanksgiving. He had already eaten so much his sides were pooching out. When I had left through the front door, he had jumped from the back porch, through the storm door screen that I had raised earlier, the screen door material poking out in stark confirmation.

I grabbed the broom and went after him. Out the door and down the steps and he still dragged the turkey by the leg into the yard. He was waddling with every step. Fortunately, he was still too fast for me and I couldn't catch him, but he finally stopped anyway. I was too tired to kill him, so I just sat down in the yard and started blubbering and feeling sorry for myself.

Ronnie was home by now with our friends. They were all laughing so hard they were hysterical. Somehow it didn't seem funny to me until later. I thought about the three invitations I had turned down.

We ate all the other food that fortunately hadn't been on the table. And the dressing had chicken in it so it was enough. And then we had pie and ice cream. That was the best pie I had in a long time. So, Thanksgiving ended on a happy note.

Poor Uppie was forgiven. He didn't want much to eat for a few days, but he came around. I was worried about him at first. He ate almost an entire turkey.

After the mess was cleaned up and the drama was over, I made a note to shut the back door and leave it shut while I was cooking at Christmas. And I think ham sounds good this time. Do you think a dog could eat a whole ham? I don't think I will chance it.

Possum and Grits, Oh My

Forget the grits, without a doubt, this story belongs to the possum.

Years ago, I had a lot of cats. And for some odd reason, the cats had cats. At dinner time my cats brought home friends, just like your kids do when you have planned a meal for four people and six extra bodies show up at your table. Well, it was the same for my cats. The more the merrier. After all, ' life happens'.

Somewhere along the line the cats began inviting a few possums to dinner. The first time I noticed anything odd was at feeding time one night when I happened to glance out my sliding glass door and saw a really ugly cat with a hairless tail, sitting in the middle of one of the food bowls. A quick note here, I didn't have my glasses on at the time, but they all seemed happy, so I didn't investigate the dinner guest. A night or two later, on closer inspection I realized it was indeed not a cat but a quite brazen possum. I let it dine that night too, but

I did notice its sharp teeth gleaming in the moonlight. After dinner it moved on.

The possum and cats soon had a close kinship. My cats love everyone and it became routine that they would frequently invite the possum to dine. So be it I thought, there is always room for one more at my house. I wasn't quite ready for the next part of the adventure, however.

You know sometimes in the middle of the night when you are snug and comfy in your soft warm bed and nature calls you to get up and trot all the way to the bathroom? No matter how hard you try to resist getting up, those kidneys just mock you and laugh? Well, it was one of those nights. What has this got to do with your story, you say? I'm getting there.

I slowly, but defiantly rolled out of bed, made the routine trip down the hall and turned on the light. Another note, I don't always turn on a light when I get up, as I am like a sonar detector in the darkness. So, I am not sure what made me flip the switch on, but looking back, I am certainly glad that I did.

There in the hazy, fluorescent glow of my otherwise sparkling bathroom was a site to behold. Smack in the middle of the toilet bowl, in all its furry glory was the cat food eating possum! How ever he had eaten his last kibble. He was stone cold dead! Drowned, in the toilet! It was a sight to behold, but one you don't want to remember. How he came to be in my bathroom and met his cruel fate is a mystery for the ages.

The next step was fishing him out. All I could find to remove him was a bent metal coat hanger, but we eventually got outside. But first, I admit, I did take a picture. Might be a bit ghoulish, but no one is going to believe a possum drowned in your toilet on your word. So, I took my picture and would show it to you today except for showing a little respect for the deceased.

After all was taken care of and I finally got back in my bed, the event kept playing over in my head. I began thinking if I hadn't turned on the light and he had only been getting a drink or playing possum, what might have happened? I also envisioned if I had to go to the emergency room at the hospital where I work. Oh my. The thoughts that come to you at three in the morning.

Sometimes you just know that the good Lord is with you in whatever form you perceive him to be, and is truly watching over you! I buried Mr. Possum in my flower bed where my cats hang out.

Rest in peace Mr. Possum. I hope you made it to possum heaven and that they have lots of good cat food there.

Lucifer and the Ice Chest

Many years ago, when my marriage was new and we were still learning things about each other, there was the 'cat' I inherited along with my new husband.

The 'cat' was already a resident of the apartment when I came into the picture. This enormous midnight-black tom cat was named Lucifer and let there be no doubt, he lived up to his name.

One never knew where Lucifer might be hiding upon arrival home, but one thing for certain, he had a penchant, like many of his cat cousins, for clawing on things. This little habit kept him in trouble a good deal of the time, and nothing seemed to stop him from his daily shredding adventures. Whether you punished him, ignored him, loved him or joined him made no difference to Lucifer. His job, as he saw it, was to destroy anything and everything he took a fancy to, and he would make sure to get the job done, even if he had to wait until you left the premises, or until you were asleep.

This line of thought brings me to the event. Since we were newlyweds, we didn't have a lot of money to spend on expensive things, but we did ok. We had purchased a cheap, Styrofoam ice chest to transport cool drinks and such for picnics, get togethers or weekend parties. Also, the apartment refrigerator was quite small and didn't always accommodate things we needed to store. So, the usual place for the ice chest came to be in a spot beside the refrigerator in the small kitchen.

Lucifer took an instant shine to the Styrofoam ice chest and with concentrated attentiveness, began the process to claim it as his own. We now continually moved the ice chest, but he would find it. Many times, here after we were wakened from a sound sleep by eerie night time sounds emanating from the kitchen or where ever the chest was stored, even in a closet, as Lucifer assaulted the defenseless ice chest. This went on for perhaps a month and nothing would stop Lu from his stealthy attacks. During his combat missions, a hellish noise would arise in the apartment that I compared to what I imagined Edgar Allen Poe must have been writing about in his garish tales.

Then one night . . . I awoke to a familiar raspy, scratching noise, but something was different. It was around 3 a.m. and Steve was nowhere to be found. I laid still listening for a few seconds and heard scuffling. I jumped out of bed, afraid there might be an intruder and slid down the hall in the darkness. Suddenly things became all too clear.

There in the beaming bright light of the kitchen stood Steve, naked and holding the ice chest over his head and shaking it. Droplets of water were spilling out on to the floor. He saw me and calmly said, "You might want to step back a bit". As I was adjusting to reality, all hell broke loose as an immense blur of wet fur went flying by my head! It let out the most furious, deafening yowling cat screechhh you have ever heard in your life, and every single hair on his body was erect as all four paws tore at the air!
Lucifer, had been in the ice chest with about a half inch of water. He kept flying around the room at race track speeds and I swear after he finally stopped, there were cat tracks on the sides of the walls. Hell, hath no fury like a pissed off cat!

I was mad at Steve, but I found myself laughing so hysterically I slid down the wall. Lucifer didn't think it was so funny and it was about a week before he would let me pet him again. Meanwhile I was wondering what I might have gotten myself into with this marriage. But I pretty much figured out that night that life would never be dull or boring.

And Lucifer? He became the sweetest, loving cat that I treasured dearly, and fathered many little Lucifers. He stayed with us until he was very old and crossed the rainbow bridge to cat heaven. And though he never let up on his exceedingly mischievous nature, I made a quiet observation that he never went near an ice chest again. I miss you, Lu.

The Birthday Girl

Did you ever go to a party and think it was so wonderful that you wanted to have one just like it? How about when you were six years old and about to be seven?

The party bug hit me one late winter day when I attended a friend's birthday party. It was the first real party I had ever been to in my young life, and to me it was amazing. So many kids were there, and there was a cake with candles on it, Kool-Aid with little paper umbrellas in the glasses, lots of games to play and presents, and getting to play all afternoon. What, could ever be better? I was hooked. I even learned the birthday song!

I decided then and there that I was going to have a birthday party and I wanted one just like this. My birthday was a whole four months away though in April. That seemed like forever! It was the weekend now though, and I would think about the party later. Today was not a school day and we were free until Monday. Right now, I just wanted to spend time with my sweet, beautiful mother. She worked all week and I didn't get to see her much until the weekend. By the time we were done with supper every night, it was about time for me to go to bed. So, weekends were the best.

Days went by quickly and it was well into late March when I decided to start inviting people to my party. I had never had a party, and I didn't know what all to do, but I knew I had to ask some people to come. I asked a couple of people if they would come and they liked the idea, and then it seems I asked a whole lot of people to come. By now, the calendar had creeped through the first week of April and my birthday was on the fifteenth. The problem with all my planning was, I forgot to tell anyone in my family that we were having my party and we were now seven days away from the big day!

Things started to get a little interesting when a friend's mother stopped by the house one day after school and asked my grandmother, who lived with us, what time the party was on Saturday? Well, that got things rolling. Grandma asked me what did I know about a birthday party on Saturday? So, I told her my whole plan. She seemed quite impressed. She couldn't wait to tell my mom when she got home from work. It was kind of like the fourth of July after that. There was some loud talking they tried not to let me hear, but I got the general idea that I had messed up.

A small child doesn't realize things like space, resources, time and money can all come into play in an event, but it became rather clear that day. Though they never let me know there was any problem, I felt it, and I realized, yes, I had really messed up. We lived in a tiny housed that five people shared, my grandmother, grandfather. mother, brother and me. Mom worked five, and sometimes five and a half days a week, and took care of everyone. She had a heart as big as a house and the faith and determination to move mountains. In fact, she frequently wore a necklace that had a single mustard seed in a tiny glass bubble, to remind her, that if you have complete faith, even as tiny as a mustard seed, you can indeed move mountains. So, in spite of me, she smiled, hugged me really tight, kissed the top of my head and said the party was on. I will never forget that day. That hug meant more than any party ever could.

Saturday the 15th came and somehow everything came together. Everything was setup in the backyard for the party. There was a big, beautiful cake that my grandma had made, bunches of games planned and there were even lots of ballons of every color. Now, it was time for people to start arriving.
About that time, the wind picked up and a rain storm came rolling in quicker than anyone could have imagined. So, everything got hurriedly

moved into our tiny living room. I don't know how we crowded everything and everyone in, but no one seemed to care about the space. Everyone sang the birthday song to me, and I was on cloud nine. We had cake, complete with candles and Kool-Aid. We even got the little umbrellas in our glasses, and I got some presents. We played all afternoon. I still remember it like it happened yesterday, but that was many moons ago. I remember watching my mom that day. She was so pretty and was laughing and smiling, with no worries for at least a few hours.

So that was the party for the birthday girl. For some reason, I can't recall another birthday party ever. But that was all right with me, because at the age of seven, I had the best birthday anyone could ever have.

Grandpa's Retirement Adventures

My grandpa, Earl Gentry was an interesting and intelligent man. In my young years, he was a retired barber, who did not want to be retired. He also got bored easily, so that did not make for a good combination. It wasn't his plan to retire at all, but in his younger years he was in a car fire where he was trapped inside and suffered severe burns to one of his legs. At that time medicine was not what it is today and the trauma was so bad, they told him he would never walk again. Those folks didn't know Earl's spirit. He never let it stop him. It just slowed him a bit. And no matter what, he always had a smile for everyone and a quick wit that could be hilarious at times.

Earl was born in 1893 and lived a great deal of his life in Prentiss County, Mississippi. His father was James R. Gentry, a school teacher/farmer who worked from sunrise to sunset at one duty or another. Family stories tell that Earl would cry to go to school with James, as he wanted to spend more time with his father. Earl was only a little fellow then, but to stop him from crying, James would let Earl play with his violin all day (in the South it's mostly referred to as a fiddle).

Somehow, by himself, Earl learned to play that fiddle and wouldn't stop until he had mastered it. By the age of twelve, he was playing with the older men in the community and they persuaded him to play in some Old Time Fiddler's Contests, which he promptly won. He became well known around the area for his playing ability. He picked up most things in life pretty easily and was a fast learner and it was a good thing, as he ended up having to take care of his many brothers and sisters after his parents both passed away at early age.

Earl soon met the love of his life, Ildra Mullennix. She told me once that she fell in love with him the first time she saw him at age five. They were married in the back of a wagon, and the rest is history. They had one daughter, Christine. It truly was a magical love and they spent the rest of their lives together.

Earl farmed a lot to keep food on the table for his brothers and sisters, but as they all began to come of age, he decided to go to barber college. He got his license and found he really liked barbering and became proficient at it. He was asked to teach students and accepted the challenge. One of his exams had students shave a balloon with a sharp straight razor.

He was always telling odd tales of things he had encountered in his barber shop. One memory is of a customer who came regularly to his shop in downtown New Albany, Mississippi. The customer was laid back comfortably in his chair with his feet crossed, and was about to receive a straight razor shave, when Earl noticed something odd about the man's feet. Something didn't look quite right. Although the man in the chair had his feet crossed his shoes were still side by side, left and right. It turned out that the man was wearing his shoes on the wrong feet to even out the heels on his shoes. Of course, the man was also known to be a bit of a skin-flint.

There are so many tales I could tell here, but I was beginning to tell you about boredom during retirement and how it can be a tiny bit dangerous.

You have to know at the start, Earl was a poster child for things happening to him, and not all of those were good things. But no matter what, he always kept a smile on his face, a happy in his heart and had the most amazing, dry sense of humor. He could also just look at the sky and tell you within a few minutes, the time of day. He also read the clouds and could tell you what the weather was about to do. He taught me how to look for wind in the clouds. I think most of this came from his many years as a farmer, and working in the fields. And he knew all the birds and their calls. He especially loved Mockingbirds and he told me they told each other stories about the things they saw and that's what they were doing when they made all those different sounds.

But again, the retirement thing.

Grandpa decided he was going to take up gardening in our tiny back yard. He said he wanted to feel useful again at something, and wanted to help out the family. One memory that I remember clearly is of him as he attempted to clean out his little summer garden so he could plant some cool weather things for fall. His plan was to simply pull up some dying okra plants to make room for mustard greens and other things. He reached down at the bottom of one plant and gave it a tug. It came out cleanly so he moved to the next one. Once again it came right up. Then, he hit a stubborn plant that he swore had roots to China. He gave it a tug. It didn't budge. He tried again, not coming out. But instead of getting a shovel or other tools, he just kept fighting with it. Then, a piece of it came up and he was envisioning victory, so he went in for the kill. He tugged a couple of times and all of a sudden, he started stumbling backwards with the plant and a huge root ball of dirt in his hands. He couldn't let go while stumbling backwards and all of a sudden, he went head over heels still holding the huge plant in both hands. He landed flat of his back with a loud thud, and I thought I heard a swear word. It was a site to behold. He just lay there, all covered in dirt until my grandmother, stuck her head out the back door and yelled, “Earl, what in the world are you doing?” He still didn’t move right away. I think it knocked the breath out of him. Ildra came out in the yard to see about him, and gave him a hug when she helped him get up. And that was it for the day. Next day he got out the hoe and shovel. With a little more effort, his autumn garden turned out really well.

Another yard memory concerned a small woodpile in the back yard. This pile had slowly accumulated over a period of time. It wasn’t really that bad, it was just messy and needed to be cleaned out. Earl decided to clean it one day and set about his task. It was his mission for the day. He decided a garden hoe would do the best job of chopping and cleaning, so he chose it, but left the rake laying a few feet away in case he needed it. The plan was to get it all in a manageable pile and pick it up or maybe just burn it. The thought had never occurred to him that something might be inhabiting the woodpile.

He had been working for a few minutes, chopping with the hoe around the edges trying to pull it all into a single pile. He thought he heard something, but by then, it was too late. Suddenly, out of holes in the ground, they came. Bees! Big bees! Usually, this type of bee is pretty docile, but Earl had really ticked them off, and they were quite angry at being disturbed. The whole wad of them launched at grandpa at once. He tried to run, and was doing pretty good at first, but his feet just wouldn't cooperate. He ended up running backwards and swinging at them with his hoe. One stung him right between the eyes, as he was still backing up. Others followed. But that was nothing compared to him stepping on the rake that was still laying in the yard, as it swung up and WHAM, hit him hard in the middle of his face where he had just been stung. That took him to the ground, where the bees continued to sting.

Once again, grandma heard the commotion and when she saw what
was happening. Out she came with some kind of bug spray that allowed them to both get back in the house. She promptly doctored his injuries, but that wood pile stayed around for a long, long time.

So many stories and memories, both good and bad. I can't wait to see
him again one day. Love you grandpa!

Bank Robbery and Chaos

June sixth began as a clear, blue, cloudless morning. Such are many mornings in this quiet town in north Mississippi. It was around nine a.m. and the town was just beginning to stir.

On a street called Varsity, behind the local music store, the data processing department for the local hospital was also coming to life for the day. This department had been temporarily housed offsite, as they were waiting for a new permanent location to be completed.

The back door of this facility faced east toward the main four lane thoroughfare which was about a block or so away. In the area between the building and the four lane was a huge parking lot with, an independent drive-up ATM machine, a Fred's Dollar Store and all the way across the parking lot was a branch bank and a tiny loan company. And across the street was a discount salvage store. Back at the data building, there were woods on the west side that ran the entire length of the building.

It was Tuesday, and around 9 a.m. a pickup truck pulled up to the glass back door. This door was where packages would be delivered for the business or relatives of employees could stop by if there was a need. The man inquired of one of our employees. She came to the door and her visitor was her stepfather. He hurriedly asked her to call the police as he didn't have a phone available to him. He was in pursuit of a man on foot, who was clutching something big in a large towel. He had seen the man come out of the bank. When the man on foot saw the employee and her stepfather talking at the door, he took the opportunity to run into the woods behind the building. He soon realized that other people were watching him in the woods from their office windows, so he ran back out to the parking lot.

The relative in the truck suddenly took off again. The employee, Wanda, thought the person in the woods had previously robbed her stepfather, so when she saw him running through the parking lot again, out the door she went running after the man with the towel. As it turned out. The running man had just robbed the branch bank across the parking lot; however, no one actually knew this at the time. Wanda still thought he had robbed her stepfather, as he made his business deposits daily at that bank, so she continued running after him and then two more of us go after Wanda, myself and my friend Susan. We are all running and screaming as we see the man now trying to cross Varsity drive, the street which runs in front of the data center. When we see him, we realize what he has in the towel is stacks of money!

So, across the street the bank robber goes, with us still chasing him and each other, still yelling and screaming all sorts of strange things. Wanda has not seen her stepfather again since he took off the second time in his truck and she was frantic that something might have happened to him.

When the three of us got across the street, we realize the robber has gone into the store on the corner. In the mean-time another man in this parking lot has joined us in the chase. The store the robber ran into is an old salvage discount store. As we start to go in, we actually start to think, wondering if the robber might have a weapon. Before now, he was too busy holding the towel full of loot with a death grip, to worry too much about it. We didn't know, however, what he might do in the store if cornered. Thankfully, we didn't have to worry, as about that time every police car in our town showed up and took over.

The police had brought a couple of canine teams with them, and promptly turned them loose in the building. The robber had hidden in a half-empty storage bin, under some merchandise and was quickly apprehended by police and their canine officers. Most of the money was recovered and returned to the bank.

It was later told by a reporter, that when the man was arrested, he said to please not let anyone else scream at him, that those women were crazy.

And us? We went back to work and tried to live down the day. It's not every day you get to chase a bank robber during work hours.

We got laughed at a lot, but none of us cared. Wanda's stepfather was all right and that was good enough for us. The police came by to visit us the next day and actually thanked us for helping out in the chaos. And life returned to normal, that is as normal as it gets around us.

Thrill Hill and Summer Fun

In my old neighborhood, there were two tall hills. Both were on city streets, if you could call our small town back then a city. Kids were drawn to those hills and streets like magnets, with parents continually yelling, stay out of the street or you're going to get hurt! That reminder would last for about an hour or so and then we would be back out there again.

There were several fun things to do on those hills, the first of course was flying down as fast as you could go on a bicycle. If you got off the hill fast, you could coast for at least two blocks. We would have races with a lot of the other kids and it was fun, as long as you didn't crash a bike and that did happen occasionally. We usually had some good cuts and scrapes too when that happened. Fortunately, in truth, there was very little traffic back then and someone was always watching for the cars.

One summer there was the go cart. It was not like the fancy and expensive go karts you could buy today. I don't remember where it came from or who built it, but it was more like a home-built soap box derby machine than an actual go kart. It was totally made of wood except for the wheels, with a rope to steer it. An accident waiting to happen? You bet. This was pretty much a thing for the boys. I knew I couldn't control it. But the boys seemed to have a knack for it, most of the time, and a lot of fun coming down the hills flying. It didn't have an engine or brakes. It was just a wooden cart a lot like the Flintstones would drive. It crashed a lot, and as such, didn't last very long before having to be patched up.

Another fun activity, my favorite, was roller skating down the hills. We usually stuck to the smaller hill in front of the house for skating, but I have been known to dare devil it down the big hill about three blocks over. You have to know too that roller skating, roller blading or whatever you may call it today has come a long way. With my old skates, you would, wear regular shoes, insert your foot between two clamps at the end of the skates and use your skate key to adjust it to the preferred tightness to hold your foot tightly in the skate clamps. The key also adjusted the skate underneath if you needed to make your skates longer or shorter. You then strapped the leather strap around your ankles and zoom, you were dare-devil ready.

I absolutely loved to skate. I finally wore the metal wheels out so that they had dimples in the wheels!

My favorite thing to do was to stop dead -still by doing 180-degree turns. What a rush that was.

On one particular day, I decided to go over to the big hill. I don't remember who was with me, or if anyone was. I sometimes went alone. I climbed to the top of the hill and made sure there was no traffic. Zoom. Off I went getting faster and faster and about midway, I hit a big rock. Wham! I turned a flip and landed on my backside, but that didn't stop the forward motion. I had so much momentum going that I continued sliding the rest of the way down thrill hill and into the intersection! I was fortunate indeed that there was no traffic, as I couldn't get up for a minute. When I did manage to get up, the whole back of my pants was in shreds and missing some spots. I sure had a lot of explaining to do when I walked the three blocks home and my grandma caught me sneaking in the back door.

Later I got into roller blading, but that was quite a few years later and I was a lot less dare devil by then. It was still fun, but just not the same.

In the summertime the city would annually tear up our playground on the hill as they were always repaving our street as the town began to grow. That was actually a bonus for us kids. The city would not just pave over the old asphalt in those days; they would actually dig the street up all the way down to the gas lines. Then they piled dirt up in what was the center of the street. Then the city placed a bunch of smudge pots on the dirt to keep drivers from running off in the huge holes. So instead of running up and down the hills, when the city workers left for the day, we would all go sit in the dirt in the middle of the street by the glow of the smudge pots. After dark we would tell stories or just talk, until we had to go inside for the night.

One night, when the street was totally dug up, and we were sitting by the glow of the smudge pots, we saw an old man in a white suit leaning against a utility pole. He was about half a block down the street. We were all wondering who he was and where he came from, and then, he just wasn't there anymore. I will never know where he went, he just disappeared. When we looked back, he was gone, so we always said he was our Civil War ghost. We knew every person in the neighborhood, so I don't know who or what that might have been or how he could have gotten out of there so fast on foot with the entire street torn up.

On thing for sure, life was never dull on our little corner of the street or on thrill hill.

Tupelo Saturdays – Downtown

Mural Downtown Tupelo

Saturdays during my childhood were the best! My brother and I got to spend the whole day with our mother. She worked Monday through Friday, but she made Saturdays our special day. Most Saturdays we went to downtown Tupelo to window shop, get a hot dog, buy groceries, go to a movie, or whatever came up. We didn't have a car, so just before noon we would catch the city bus in front of our house for an adventure.

As we usually got to town around lunchtime, our first stop was usually the TKE Drug Store. TKE stood for Thomas, Kincannon and Elkin. The drug store was already a business that had been in Tupelo for generations. They had most anything a body could want. There was a lunch counter, pharmaceuticals, sundries, magazines and books including comics, and the store even carried school supplies and workbooks children needed for school in the Fall.

To me, the lunch counter was the best part of the store. We seldom got to eat out. Most meals during these days were cooked at home. so, getting to eat downtown was a special treat. And the hot dogs seemed magical to us small folks. Of course, potato salad went with those hot dogs and in Tupelo, there was actually a rivalry between two drug stores for who had the best potato salad. The other drug store was T & S Pharmacy. They were located over the hill a couple of blocks away, but since we were closer to the bus stop, we usually ended up at TKE. Both places had excellent potato salads. The T & S Pharmacy building had some doctor's offices in it, so on those days that one might have to visit a doctor, their lunch counter was available to get a bite to eat. TKE was my favorite as I loved to eat my hotdog and then go look at comics.

Next, we might possibly wander across the street and go to Kermit's Bakery for a small treat. They had all kinds of cookies, cakes and baked goods, so it was also a fun place to visit, and a favorite.

If we decided to go to a movie, we would walk back across the street to the Tupelo Theater, or head to an afternoon movie at the Lyric Theater across from the courthouse. The Lyric was a Tupelo staple as well. It was actually used as a morgue in the horrible Tupelo tornado of April 1936. We rarely did movies though as there was always so much we needed to do.

Back on Spring Street we would head north toward our grocery store destination, but along the way there was Ben Franklin Five and Dime Store, Debs Dollar Store that also sold shoes. Next door was a hardware store. I have forgotten the name of the store, but they had big dusty windows with seeds and boots and axes in the windows. And I can still smell the myriads of fertilizers with their pungent aromas.

Across the street was the Lee County Courthouse. A place to do business during the regular work week covering everything from taxes to car tags. It was a beautiful old building, set among old trees that had benches of old men, most in overalls spitting tobacco juice on the sidewalks and telling many a tall tale. The courthouse was also rumored to be haunted, though I never personally encountered anything there.

Finally turning left past the courthouse was Page's Grocery. Mr. Page was a jolly man and always had a friendly greeting for us. We actually spent the bulk of our day there, but I loved going to the grocery store. This store was where my brother finally learned the difference between a head of lettuce and a cabbage. He was usually super smart, but there was something about cabbage that didn't click with him at first. After all our groceries had been processed and put in giant brown paper bags, we would walk back to the bus stop with all our packages and wait for the next bus. There was a large bench on the corner, so it was fun waiting on the bus and people watching.

On one Saturday when the bus came, my brother got up and left the bag of groceries he had sat down beside the bus bench while we waited. I don't remember the details of how we got them back, I just know we did. Mom had been in a panic mode, as that was all the money we had for groceries that week. But it all worked out for us. People were really honest back then. Some still are today, but I can't imagine someone leaving groceries somewhere today and them still being there when you returned. But lots of folks are thankfully still that honest.

Anyway, this was a typical Saturday afternoon, Always, a treat and such precious time with my mother. What a wonderful time and place to grow up.

The Motorcycle

The crazy things I did in my twenties was sometimes a sight to behold. I was out of high school, my grandmother who had raised me had just passed away and my mother had just remarried her first husband twenty years after they had divorced. She moved to California and all that remained was myself, my brother and a tiny house in Tupelo, Mississippi. My brother had a job, and I had a part time job and also sold arts and crafts at weekend, craft shows around the area.

Transportation to simply get around town had become problematic. The city bus system had quit running several years ago, taxis were too expensive, And I had done my share of walking everywhere. My brother had an old Camaro, but he needed it every day to go to work. So, I decided I would find some cheap form of transportation.

I hit upon the idea of a motorcycle. I don't know why I didn't just get a bicycle, but I wanted something that moved under its own power. Did I have one in mind, no. Did I know how to ride one, no. Did I have enough money to get one, not sure.

But how hard could it be? When you are young you just go for it. So, I set about looking for a motorcycle. We didn't have the internet, or too many ways to search for items back then, but there was a community want ads paper that came out every week, that listed tons of items for sale. One week during the first part of summer I was reading the ads and, there it was! Honda 125, Marks, Mississippi, $800 and a phone number. I called my best friend, Diane and talked to her about it. Then I called Marks.
Diane always had a nice car and a heart as big as a house, and she was always more than generous on taking me places when she could. So, the next day that I was off, and my brother was working, we took off. Not just a few miles, but to Marks, Mississippi! It was about ninety-five miles and close to two hours to get there. We thought this might be a wild goose chase, so we were ill-prepared to actually buy the bike.

When we got there, I loved the tiny little bike. Problem was I couldn't ride it home if I bought it, as I didn't know how to ride it, yet! But we bought it anyway and somehow loaded it up in the trunk of her car!

Yes, we were crazy, but we had faith. So, we were homebound with a motorcycle in the trunk with the front wheel hanging partially out. But it was in there.

When we got home, we managed to get it out of the trunk and onto the driveway. To me, it was beautiful. I didn't know how my brother was going to take it, but when he got over the shock of what we had done, he was actually fine with it. He did ask how I planned to ride it? What a concept. Since I had just spent all my money, I knew I had to make this work, but I had a plan.

Next day. I rolled it up to the elementary school about half a block from my house. It was summer, so the parking lot was empty and a big space almost the size of half a football field was next to that. I was by myself, but determined. I cranked it, went through the gears with my foot and this was the moment. I slowly tried to move forward in a big circle. I was really wobbly at first, but with every circle I got a tiny bit better and my confidence grew. This just might work. I did the same thing for the next few days, but I was riding it home now and felt in control.

Later that day I rode to my friend's house. She laughed and laughed at me, but was truly happy for me. I rode it back to my house, and the rest is history. Everybody laughed at me because it was so small, but so was I and it just fit me. I rode that little bike for years and had some great adventures, but I learned the hard way to wear a helmet.

I was riding just behind our house and there was a tree with a low hanging branch. I had been by it dozens of times, but this day, something happened and I got too close to the tree and wham. I was knocked off my little bike and my head hit the ground and the bike ended up on the side of the road in a ditch. The bike wasn't hurt, but I had a big goose bump on the back of my head for a couple of days. As soon as it went down, I bought a helmet. The helmet didn't help the day I ran under the clothes line though, but at least I didn't hurt my head.

There is nothing compared to riding free as the wind on a quiet, curvy road. In town however, things can sometimes get scary as people really don't watch out for bike riders, or perhaps they just don't see them.

The first time my future husband saw me, I was riding my little bike. He had no idea who I was and I didn't even see him that day but he saw and remembered me, because a few months later we met actually met in person and he said "you're that girl with the motorcycle". Turns out that time he saw me he was helping someone repair a roof. That's why I didn't see him.

My later-in-life brother-in-law rode my little bike and locked the engine up. She never got a chance to run again, as my then father-in-law quietly had her hauled off to the junkyard. It broke my heart, but it happened and that was that.

I surely would love to ride one more day on my little bike. We certainly had a lot of fun.

The Rocking Chair Marathon

Long ago, there was the Sears Mall on south Gloster Street in Tupelo, Mississippi. It opened to the public in late 1969 or early1970 and had a pretty long history as a favorite of residents, but as the town began to grow and expand, most of the retail businesses left in search of bigger deals or else closed their doors. At that point in time, other types of clients began to move in. Today it is mostly medically related offices.

Back in the seventies though, the old Sears Mall (actual name Tupelo Mall) was a fun place to be and a great place to shop or grab a bite to eat. There was a Sears store at one end of the mall and a McRae's at the other end, with all sorts of other smaller shops and eateries up and down the row. The mall also hosted occasional events, one being a Rocking Chair Marathon, which took place several times over the years.

To enter the contest, applicants had to put their applications in a box and have their name drawn to be able to participate. But first, they had to sign a statement that they had no disabilities or known health problems before they could be considered for entry. Officials, then drew ten or twelve names as entries, but I can't honestly say I remember the exact number. Upon being selected you then drew a number out of another box that determined what chair you would rock in. All the chairs were donated by local furniture stores for the event, so each chair was very different. Rules stated that you could not leave the area except on your five-minute break, that was your bathroom break, and that five minutes came around once an hour. You also had to have a continuous rocking stride, and if you started slowing down, officials would slap a ruler down by the side of your chair, and you had to maintain at least that size rocking motion to stay in the contest.

Why do all this? There were three prizes. First place was five hundred dollars; second place was three hundred and third place was two hundred dollars. Not much in today's money, but to a person in their twenties, forty or fifty years ago, it seemed like a lot of money for just rocking in a rocking chair. And so, it began.

It seems a few people had lied about being healthy and believe me, it didn't take long for that

to become quite apparent. The event started on a Thursday morning and by Friday morning about half were gone. You could have a team of folks to bring you things like food and drinks or blankets, or pillows for your back where the rocking spokes were making bruises on your back.
My best friend, Diane had also applied to enter and was chosen to be in the contest too. She was sitting far behind me though as we were sitting in a circle facing out toward the outside. Both of us were still hanging in on Saturday afternoon but I'm serious, this was tough.

On my five-minute break if I didn't have to go to the bathroom, I would lay down on a small bench and hang my head off the end to get some circulation flowing in my head. And for trying to stay awake, at one point I was counting the holes in a fly swatter. All was going fairly well until later that afternoon when the guy sitting next to me started losing his marbles. Remember, this is three days and two nights into the contest. I'm not sure if he was on medication or just sleep deprived, but he started hallucinating. The first I noticed, he asked did I see that mouse run to the top of the wall? No, I did not. After he saw several other things, he escalated his drama. At the time, he had a huge, iced cola drink in his hand and he stood up and screamed "there it is" and threw his entire drink at a man walking by and it hit him square in the chest. Pandemonium ensued as officials ran to stop the fight, but the contestant had stopped rocking so he was out.

We were down to four people now, one of which was a nurse. She also had some minor health issues that had started to take a toll on her as well. She was afraid she was going to fall out of her chair, so on her break, she had someone tie her in her chair.

Diane was doing well. Her family spent almost the entire time with her and they were a great cheering section. Saturday night I realized I was in a wee bit of trouble. I was beginning to get tunnel vision. I didn't realize it until my brother came to sit by me and I thought he had left because I couldn't see him. He was there, off to my side, but he finally had to get in front of me before I could see him. And I thought I was okay. This was the third complete day and night of no sleep.

Sunday morning, the last guy went out. He said he just couldn't take it anymore and walked off. That left the three of us. Diane, myself and the nurse. A couple of hours later, the nurse had some kind of medical meltdown. The took her off in an ambulance!

I made it until lunchtime on Sunday, where by I don't remember, but they say I got up and swore at everybody and walked off south, toward Sears. Apparently, I went outside the south door at Sears where they had several boats of some kind. I laid down on the concrete by one of the boats and I was out like a light. Nobody came to look for me, so I laid there until my brother got help and came to find me. At some point though, I had apparently walked across the street and down the block to Jack's Hamburgers, as someone saw me there, and then I had gone back to my concrete bed at Sears and went back to sleep.

Meanwhile, Diane had been declared the winner of the five hundred dollars. I didn't care squat about the money at that point, but later I was happy for her. and I apologized for swearing, though I have no memory of that except what I was told. I got my three hundred dollars, second place prize, a couple of days later, but somehow, I wasn't very excited.

So bottom line, that was the end of rocking chair contests at the Tupelo Mall! All the crazy people went home, and life returned to normal.

Diane and I both bought our rocking chairs from the furniture stores to remember to NEVER do such a crazy thing again. Although we didn't do that again, being best friends, life gave us a backpack full of other amazing adventures and memories.

In memory of my forever friend, Diane Petty Dobbs

The Karate Agenda

When you are alone most of the time, you like to think you would be able to protect yourself if the need came along. This idea led to another adventure in my life, when I decided that I was going to take karate lessons.

I went to a local class one night to observe and by the time it was over I was signed up to start the next week. Karate is not for the faint of heart, or the out of shape,if you are either, you won't be for long. This class, if I remember was about three hours long. It was called Tan Su Karate which is a mixed form of karate that highlights self-defense. And it is still taught in this area today.

There were basically four parts to each class. There were basic warm up exercises, calisthenics with lots of pushups and sit-ups, and lots of stretching for flexibility, there was a learning phase, which taught new movements and techniques, group practicing, and the night would end with everyone sparring with a teacher or selected partner. All degrees of belts worked out together, novice and advanced, as the teacher's thought was that if someone was to attack you, they might be a novice or an expert and you needed to be over the shock of being grabbed by anyone, so that this enabled you to use a calm head to execute an automatic response you had been trained to release.

Everyone has heard of a black belt, or advanced black belts, masters and grand masters. If dedicated, you truly never stop learning There were eight degrees of black belts in this order, years ago. I can only imagine what they went on to accomplish. These are the expertly trained fighters who can pretty much handle whatever situation comes along.

Then, there were the rest of us who were learning and went from white, advanced white, yellow, advanced yellow, blue, advanced blue, green, advanced green, brown, advanced brown, and then first-degree black belt. And that is when the learning truly begins.

The first thing we learned was respect. Our teacher made it very clear, over and over, that karate is not to hurt people for no reason, it is to defend yourself in bad situations. He told us that no matter who we were, that if we ever did anything to downgrade karate or intentionally hurt someone without due cause, that he would come and do to us whatever we did to them. Believe me you would not want sensei to come looking for you. He could definitely leave a mark. I have learned that he is a Grand Master now and that makes me so proud.

Another thing we were taught is to always try to avoid a fight or find a way out. If you could, be a diplomat, talk your way out, or if you could escape, run. But if there was no way out, get the first lick in and make it really count!

For some group practice we would break up into several groups in class and each would take turns with the others in the group chasing you. You would have to defend yourself and counter when your time came. This was another tactic to have your lessons instilled in you, so that you learned an automatic response. I don't know how they teach these days, but this helped me out of a bad situation one time in a real-life situation.

A similar exercise that I enjoyed in class was everyone in the entire class would line up, single file and the first in line would turn and face the line. Each person in the line would then, one at a time, encounter the defender. The defender would defend that person's attack and counter it. This would go on until everyone in the line had a turn at being the defender. This was some very valuable experience as you had to watch and think quickly. At the last part of each class everyone would have a chance at sparring. You did not get to choose who you would fight. It was chosen for you. This way you got used to sparring with many types of fighters and their styles. You might fight a white belt or a black belt, a man, a woman, or a young person. They might be short, tall, skinny or all muscles.

Sometimes you might be intimidated, other times not so much. Sometimes you learned some hard lessons. But it made you a better person and a better fighter. When you had met the requirements for your color of belt, there would be a test of your skills to see if you were ready to move to the next level. Sometimes you did, and this was a quite happy occasion where you would be awarded the next color belt, or a red stripe noting that you were advanced in your current belt color. There was not a set time to advance. You didn't move on until you were ready and proficient in what was taught you.

I still remember two occasions to this day when I didn't defend myself properly. On night while sparring with a brown belt, I didn't dodge a punch thrown at my face. Wham! This was a guy who had never hit a girl before, and I had never been hit in the face that hard by a fist before, and we both got a lesson. He kept saying I'm sorry, I'm sorry, and I kept telling him it was my own fault. But it was a good punch and being unexpected on my part, it was just like in the cartoons when Tom and Jerry are fighting and one gets hit over the head and sees stars. It truly rang my bell!

The other time was when I threw a round house kick at my sparring partner's head, and got the top of my foot punched just as hard as the one to my face. It actually hurt worse. Not a game for sissies.

Wherever my instructor Greg is these days, I hope he is still instilling all his amazing knowledge to others. I know that there are still eighth degree blackbelts and above coming out of this group.

I love, admire and appreciate every single one of you, as I know what goes into getting there. And thank you for the things you taught me about respect. It has stayed with me my entire life.

Ben, the Tent and the Rabbit

I'm not sure where this story is going exactly. This memory just stuck in my head as one of life's little side adventures.

Once, there was Ben. Ben was my father-in-law, but to put it mildly, he was quite a character You honestly never knew what to expect when he was around, but it was never dull. Every single day, was a rollercoaster. We'll get back to Ben soon.

Firstly though, let me explain, I truly love to go camping and hiking. I have actually only got to go a few times in my life, but every time, I went, I had a wonderful time. How ever no one else in my family today likes camping.

I kept trying to encourage everyone though, because sooner or later, I thought someone would go with me. I can't see going to the woods by myself. Some folks love that, but to me, it's about family and enjoying each other's company. Anyway, this is the very reason I bought the tent. I just kept believing.

Yes, I bought a tent, a nice one that would accommodate multiple persons. It was blue, and new and ready to travel. But still, no one would go camping with me. Well, my tent sat around for a couple of years, just rolled up in the corner. Still no takers. I was now about ready to actually go by myself.

Then one day, a friend of my husband's came by and was talking to him about going on a hunting trip out West. I think it was to Colorado or somewhere in that vicinity. As they were talking, it came up that he was going to have to buy a tent for the trip, as he didn't have one. One thing led to another and Steve volunteered my new tent for their hunting trip! I was not very happy about that, but what the heck. It wasn't being used, and that would have been a little selfish.

The trip happened, and they all had fun, but as trips go, as sometimes happens with friends, the tent didn't make it back right away. In fact, it was pretty wet and getting moldy lying around in his yard. Anyway, it came home in due time and we decided to make the best of it, clean it up and store it again.

At the time, we were living next to my in-laws and we thought nothing of setting it up in the yard between our houses, to thoroughly, dry out and air out. A few days went by and I thought it should be dried out enough by now to take it down and put it back in storage. As I walked up to start taking the tent down, I noticed a big hole in one side. That hadn't been there when we put the tent out to dry! And everything that had been zipped up was not zipped anymore. I walked over, looked in and, oh my.

Apparently, at some point, maybe after a beverage or two, Ben had decided to put a rabbit in the tent! Where he got the rabbit, how it came to be in his possession, I don't know. Why he thought it was a good idea to make him a home in the tent, that's another mystery. But he certainly did.

Sometime later, the neighbors pack of dogs found Mr. Rabbit's new home. It must have been awful. They made an unwelcome visit and made a big, nasty hole in the side of the tent to visit him. There was, poop and all manner of nasty, disgusting things everywhere inside. When we said something about the rabbit hotel, we were told we could clean it up and patch it with duct tape and it would be just like new. Sigh . . ..

No duct tape, no cleaning for me. That was all she wrote. I gave up and the tent went to the garbage, and to this day, I have never been camping again, or even wanted to go.

I just hope that Mr. Rabbit made it to rabbit heaven. I surely hope all my lost animals are there, heaven that is; and waiting for me. I miss every single one.

The Treehouse

In my mind's eye, I can still see the treehouse. The crooked ladder, the crooked limbs, the solid, but uneven floor, the red dirt kicking up on a windy day, when a long, dry summer had parched the Earth. I can feel the rough wood on my backside, as I sat on the dusty floor, leaned up against her walls, with a feeling of safety; like being in your mother's arms on a bad day. I can hear kids laughing and making secret plans. And although it's been around seventy years, the memories are strong and sparkling and bring my soul a sense of peace I've never found anywhere else, except maybe in a midnight prayer. It was good.

I'm not sure who actually built the treehouse. It was just there when a generation of us kids came along. It was located across a dirt road behind our house, in a pasture, full of cows. Cows that loved to come up under the trees occasionally to get out of the hot, Mississippi sun. The platform was about ten to twelve feet off the ground, but that surely felt high to the kid in me. There were days a kid might get tossed out of it, or fall out of it, for one reason or another. And of course there were some dares to jump out. No one ever got badly injured, just scrapes and bruises. I guess we just had tougher constitutions back in those days.

Parents knew about the treehouse, but I don't recall anyone's parents ever coming there. They knew where the kids were, and that was all they wanted to know. They were safe, except from each other.

My brother and his band of gypsies occupied the treehouse long before my younger bunch moved in. They were there for years and I know they had good times there too. I recall my brother letting me tag along one day. I was thrilled to be there in such amazing company, but that was the only time I ever got to go there when they ruled the day.

There was a long, low-lying limb on another tree close by. It was perfect for riding my imaginary horse. I spent hours riding off in the sunset with Hop-A-Long Cassidy and other cowboy stars.

Kids on slower days would look for civil war relics. A huge battle was fought in the area of Harrisburg many, many years ago and we actually found mini balls, and one time a belt buckle. Kids liked to tell stories, true or not about Civil Wars ghosts haunting some of the surrounding houses. Lots of ghost stories were told in the treehouse.

Actually, the whole pasture was a virtual playground for kids, with the ponds for the cows. Ponds which sometimes froze over during really cold winters and made a perfect place to shoe skate on the ice. There was even a creek close by good for sneaking a swim in the summer. You wouldn't hear of anything like that these days.

Later kids even had a wrestling ring in the tree, whereby they would actually throw each other out, pretending they were on a television wrestling show. That one got a little crazy., but the guy who started doing that actually ended up being a professional wrestler in Memphis and across the South.

But the treehouse remained the prize. You could hang there in the sunshine or the rain, in the heat or the cold, if you were lonely or wanted to tell your friends a secret. It was a place for stories. It was a place to hide candy and snacks, take a nap or observe life in the pasture. It was quiet, or it was boisterous, and it was ours. A place where you could be yourself. No conditions or hidden agendas.

I hope someday when I get to heaven that maybe God might see fit for that old treehouse to be around somewhere, for if ever there was a happy place of peace and contentment it was there.

Part II

Odd fiction

We Blend Anything

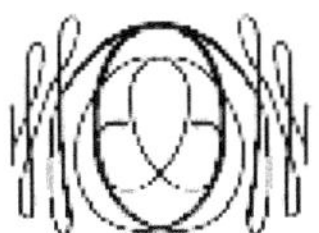

Alfred sat at the small dining table staring out the dirty window of the mobile home, listening to the shrill booming voice racing down the hall; the voice that always found him no matter where he happened to be. The same grating voice that always had some horrible nasty insult or demeaning comment just for him. It was Roberta's voice.

He often wondered what happened to the tiny slip of a girl he fell in love with, and dreamed with and wanted to spend his life with? That Roberta had died a long time ago and had been replaced by this shrieking shrew that seemed like a creature from a bad science fiction novel. "It" hated everyone and everything in sight, especially Alfred. Its hollow-eyed accusations and emasculations knew no limits.

In latter days he had tried so hard to make her happy, always putting her first, and giving up the one thing he wanted most in life, to become an accomplished chef. He wanted to be the best chef on the Gulf Coast and he knew he had the talent. He just had to get his formal training. He seemed to stay lost in that dream lately.

Two words. Katrina came! After the hurricane, life had been one gigantic struggle. They lost everything and had no place to live, no clothes, no money and no one to help. There was nothing left of the restaurant where Alfred had been employed. Only a slab of concrete marked the spot where it once stood. Jobs were scarce. And just finding food and water was a daily challenge. As a result, they came to live in the edge of a Katrina waste land on the edge of New Orleans, in a small mobile home, temporarily provided by FEMA. Alfred worked when something came along but it was slow for everyone. Days got slower and uglier. Instead of trying to appreciate what little they had acquired all Roberta did was complain and bark orders and insults and lay on her backside.

He never let anyone know how depressed he had become or how the days weighed on him. He just kept trying to make some kind of home for them, though she fought him every step of the way. Things just soured like something rotten. The love had gone, the like was waning, and he didn't know where things might go. But he just kept trying.

"Bring me a sandwich you sorry excuse for a man. It's not like you are doing anything useful...like you could BE useful, and run me some bath water I want to soak awhile, I look puffy. Can you get this right? Can you get anything right? You are such a pig...why I married you I will never know! I had to be on drugs. And hurry the hell up you slug!

The animosity she spewed was worse every day, and it never stopped. Never. He needed a break to think. She made his brain physically hurt.
Her voice was like it was scraping the skin off his body. "Please God" he mumbled under his breath. "Please help me" he continued in a half-formed prayer.

"Where's my friggin' sandwich stupid? I don't have all day like you do. Why don't you cleanup this pig sty?"

He was half way through making a sandwich when a dream began to form in his mind. He tried to push it out of his head, but it was like a red, hot flame and once the idea had formed, there was no putting it back in the box. He took her sandwich to her and she was still belting it out. He went back to the living room and crawled in the corner to the old frayed but comfortable sofa. There he fell into a deep sleep and troubled dreams.

When he awoke much later, a big full moon was shining on the water. She had gone to sleep in the tub again and he quietly sneaked out the back

door. Silence finally! Above, the stars twinkled on a black velvet canvas. It was amazing what tiny scraps of life a human could survive on he thought. He drank in fresh, deep breaths and saved the memory of this peace in
his heart.

His mind wandered to the bustling restaurant in New Orleans again. "You are a natural Alfred. As soon as you get your formal training you
will be a top chef at my place" Nico said, "Don't forget, I always have a place for you. " At that moment Alfred almost smiled.

The sun was rising and the shrieking began all over again. She was in rare form today actually spewing spittle in her anger. But today, Alfred was distracted. Nothing in this world could bother him. He had seen a commercial on television for a new type of kitchen blender. The ad said "We can blend anything! He watched, almost hypnotized as they put thing after thing in this professional blender to show how tough it was. They put in wood, glow sticks, car keys, cell phones even tubes of super glue. The blender ate everything it came in contact with using its over- sized blades and spindles. It truly blended everything! He had to have it!

It was very expensive, but Alfred already knew just how to get it. He quietly and secretly ordered it on Roberta's only credit card. It would be a month before the bill came in. "So, what" he laughed.

When it arrived a few days later, he went to town to pick it up on the excuse of buying a few groceries. She was asleep in the tub again when he got back. He unboxed it and began to play. It was whisper quiet. He was in the zone and cooked everything he could find. Then came the first blast of Roberta. "Bring me something to eat you moron".

Right then and there, Alfred's brain shorted out and spewed like the foam in a can of soda that has been shaken. He decided to make a special chocolate shake in the new blender. Soon his amazing shake was ready. He smiled.

He went to Roberta. His heart was pounding so hard he thought she might hear it. She was too busy with her stream of profanity to notice anything but the food. He had a chocolate shake and a beautifully plated sandwich. She grabbed the shake first and had gulped it halfway down before she started choking on the tooth picks, rat poison, all the medications he could find, electronic parts and metal shavings, drain cleaner and a good dash of antifreeze. It was very well blended. Her eyes started to bulge and a drop of blood came out of her mouth. She started to shake violently. He reached down, pulled her head up and said "What's the matter Berta? Cat got your tongue? " Her eyes starred wildly. As she opened her mouth to try to speak, he suddenly squirted an entire long tube of super glue in her mouth, closed her lips, and walked away.

He stayed outside for a while listening to the birds sing. Walking back to the door, later he came to himself, and was actually horrified. "How could I do that?" But at the same time, he was so relived it out weighed all other emotions. He sank to the floor in realization and when he came to, it was night. And it was very quiet

Piece by piece the blender kept chewing until there was no scrap left. What a machine he thought, as he cleaned the place to a spotless shine. He was meticulous. If there was one thing he knew how to do, it was clean. He had been doing it his entire life. He had some regrets, but Roberta had gone insane at some point. He saw that now. And he knew that her spirit could rest and be calm.

He gathered everything of value and his clean blender and made two last stops. One was to a nearby swamp where he left what few remains there were and said goodbye. Then, he stopped by an all- night pawn shop with a few items for some money to get him by. Last he heard, Nico had opened an upscale place in Austin. "Next stop Texas" he said.

He rolled down the truck windows to feel the wind in his hair and face. Then he slipped the truck into gear, turned the radio to a country station and with a smile slid out on to the waiting highway.

No trace of Roberta or Alfred was ever found; seems they simply disappeared one day. It was weeks before anyone had realized they were missing. The newspaper reported them missing, but there was no sign of foul play. Looked like they had just packed up and moved on. The mobile home was in perfect order and was returned to FEMA.

It was assumed the couple had just moved on like so many other misplaced people of the time. One neighbor said he only noticed they were gone because it was so quiet.

About George Mavis

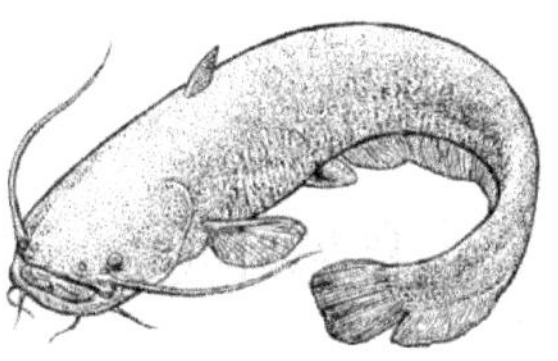

The summer heat down South had turned into an Indian summer. Lazy, still warm sunshine washed the shadowy trees, and flowers continued to bloom abundantly in a blanket of artist's colors. Emerald green grass poured over the landscape of this beautiful day, surrounding everything.

In Tarlton, Mississippi, George Mavis sat on his small overgrown patio drinking his last Bud in a can, and contemplated his less than wonderful life. What happened to him along the way to be here, on this day, in this place, alone in life, with five lousy bucks to his name until the end of the month? Truth was, he didn't really care what happened to him since Eva died.

Cancer had taken the love of his life, his precious Eva, just three short months ago and in this tiny space of time folks had already forgotten him. At first it was a packed house with neighbors bringing food and stopping by to say how sorry they were for "his loss"; the words tumbled over in his brain like heavy weights. It sounded as though they had gone for a walk and he simply lost her somewhere down the road. He knew they meant well but it made him even sadder, if that was possible.

George had just retired last year from his forty-five-year job at the hardware store. They had such wonderful dreams planned. He thought their future was at last going to be something fun and wonderful for them.

It had been a hard life. Their only son Daniel was killed in an automobile accident several years ago by a drunk driver. So much heartache and the grief almost killed them both. George had been determined to make their golden years happy ones and salvage what life they had left together. He wanted to take Eva some beautiful place she had never been before. He dreamed of taking her to a tropical island where they would walk on the beach and he would put a beautiful flower behind her ear. It would pale in comparison to her beauty though. Eva was still as beautiful as the day he met her. The way the sun played on her golden hair, the curve of her smile and the twinkle in her deep green eyes made him fall head over heels in love with her the first time he saw her all those years ago, "Oh Eva".

At this moment, George rose from his frayed patio chair with a grunt and a deep sigh. He knew sitting here was making things worse, so he decided on a whim to walk down to the lake and go fishing. His heart wasn't really in it, but at least it would be a change of scenery. He took his last gulp of beer and tossed the can.

He went into the house, which was badly in need of a good scrubbing, made himself a sandwich and filled an old water bottle with left over tea. Next, he gathered up his fishing gear and headed out the back door grabbing his last Twinkie off the counter as he headed out. It was about a mile to the lake but he figured he probably needed the exercise, so he didn't bother with the truck.

The walk actually made him feel a little better. He piled his belongings into his old boat that he kept tied at the lake and decided he would paddle out instead of cranking the engine right away. The old boat ran like a top, but he just needed to get his weight into something.

When he found his spot, George slid the boat over so he was facing west and could see the sun as it lowered in the sky. He took a deep breath and breathed in the fresh air. He cast a line and it wasn't long before a big catfish found it. He pulled in his fish, but once again, his heart wasn't in it so he gently dropped the fish back into the water and watched it swim away. "Swim home old boy, I will catch up with you another day ". He didn't like death in any form today.

He just sat in the boat for a long while, drinking in the beauty of his surroundings. It was the first time in a long time that he had allowed himself to breathe. He drank in the fresh air until he thought his lungs might burst.

He was still alive. Somehow after everything that had happened, he was still alive. His thoughts were still of Eva and Daniel, but as with Daniel, he now knew that he must choose to live or die.
He was still turning over these thoughts in his head as a low mist began to form on the lake.

The sun was setting and dusky darkness was beginning to envelop the small boat. George had been on the lake many times at night, but
he was suddenly very tired and wished he had brought his old truck. He could be home in five minutes. He turned to the back of the boat to start the engine when he heard a small voice somewhere behind him say quietly "George Mavis".

George spun around, standing at attention, almost falling into the water. He knew he was a little crazy lately, but he also knew he had definitely heard someone speak his name. A chill ran up his spine.

The voice spoke again “George Mavis”, this time a little louder with a questioning tone. In a panic he muttered “who are you? I can’t see you! “ “I am here in your boat. Don’t be frightened George Mavis.” “Call me George” he said, realizing he was talking to the air. Paralyzed with fear, he sought the end of the boat.

There sitting upright and talking was a catfish! “It really is alright George”. I threw you back in the water. I really don’t want death for anyone or anything right now.”

“And that would be because of Eva and Daniel “said the fish “and your old yellow dog Sam?” George just looked at the fish, but he couldn’t say a word. His heart exploding in sobbing tears. I need to get home he thought.

The mist continued to rise and cover the spaces just above the water. George had suddenly become grateful for the company of the fish. “Just who are you really my fish friend? “A few moments later the fish replied “I am God, George”. George could not speak. Insanity had consumed him.

"God?" You are God?" He finally said as he smiled and shook his head. "You are a cat fish or at least you look like one to me"God?

"Do you not think I can take any form I wish when it pleases me, George? I can do all things as I wish. I take many forms at times to see how people will react to trials and tasks that I send to them. I am here to give you a choice George. I know the lake is a place you sometimes find peace so I chose to meet you here."

The full moon had risen overhead. The fish form spoke one more time. "Do you believe in me George? This is a crossroad for you. You can stay here or you can come with me and find peace.

George exhaled heavily and then stammered. "This is the last thing I expected to happen today, or ever, for that matter, but I believe I choose to tag along with you, fish."

Suddenly a glow of pure white light began to envelop the bottom of the boat. Then swirling colors began to rise and light up the entire sky, and twinkle like led lights on a grand scale. Then the light surrounding George turned a rose color that radiated everywhere, and he vanished in a flash from the boat.

In the next instant George awoke and the sun was shining in the most brilliant blue sky he had ever seen. He suddenly felt warm sand on his bare feet and between his toes and he felt years younger. He thought I must finally have had a good night's sleep.

Then he realized he was in the most beautiful place he had ever seen and he felt so at peace. There were tropical flowers everywhere. He thought, what is this place as he glanced down the beach.

His heart suddenly leaped out of his chest as not fifty feet away he saw them. She turned to look at him and smile, golden hair flashing in the sun. Next to her she had her arm wrapped around a tanned young man, and there was a pretty girl talking to the young man, but he didn't recognize her. But he did realize that was Daniel whom Eva was hugging. George reached to pick a nearby crimson flower and ran as fast as his feet and heart could carry him. And as he ran, he realized an old yellow dog was running and barking beside him. "Good boy Sam, good boy."

George Mavis Awakens

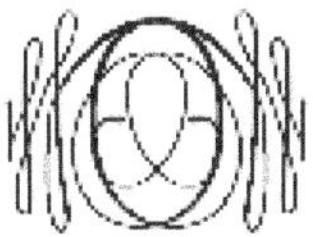

George awoke as abruptly as when he landed on the beach, or thought he landed on the beach? As the shock began to drain from his senses, he realized he had been fast asleep in his own bed. Or had he? He was so confused. How did he get here? Did he ever leave the house? He stumbled to the garage in an effort to find out what had just happened. It was so real! He could still smell Eva's sweet scent and feel the kiss she placed upon his lips and the warmth of Daniel's arms embracing him. "It was real" he muttered as he stumbled through the piles of junk lying in the floor outside the kitchen. Fear struck him as he reached for the handle. He hesitated for a brief second and threw open the door.

He quickly flipped on the switch and the dim bulb in the garage sprang to life. It was still dark out. "I know it was real" he kept repeating the words over and over as he bit his lip to stop the endless chattering. In the far corner was the familiar outline of his fishing pole and tackle. Nothing was out of place. “Oh God no” he murmured as his heart sank.

He started back through the door, his head spinning with confusion, and just then, under his bare feet, there was a crunch. As he looked down, there was a clear cellophane wrapper that had once held a Twinkie. George’s heart stopped. He grabbed the wrapper and ran into the kitchen. He poured the garbage into the floor and there was the empty Twinkie box. He did take it with him. He had eaten that Twinkie in the boat yesterday!

Suddenly a Twinkie wrapper became the most important thing in his life. But it was just a Twinkie wrapper his brain screeched. As soon as dawn broke, George was in his old truck headed to the lake. The sun was shining, not a cloud in the sky as he pulled alongside the boat launch.

Sure enough, there was his boat tied just as he previously remembered.

He walked to where the boat bobbed in the water and waded over to it. He climbed in the boat as if half expecting a miracle, or as if he expected

to be swept away or struck by lightning. But nothing happened. He sat there trying to make his mind clear or to make sense of last night. He wanted to scream to the sky, to God or to the catfish, whatever had clenched him in its grasp and then spit him out in a heap. He now began to hear himself say faintly "It was just a dream". George started to cry again. He had cried so few times in his life, it was foreign to him, yet here he was again sobbing. He threw one leg over the side of the boat to walk back to his truck and his eye caught a glimpse of something white where he thought his brown paper bag had sat yesterday. He had no idea of what was real anymore but he let his eyes wander the length of the boat. There on the floor was the white something he had seen crumpled into a ball. He hadn't noticed it previously, but he scooped it up and continued up the bank, and to his truck. It was just a stupid piece of paper so what impact could that have on his life? "Not a damn thing" he said to himself, as his mind drifted to Eva again.

Standing outside the door to his truck he un-crumpled the paper simply because it was the next step to putting this behind him. It was an old gas receipt from the bait shop down the road. But as he turned it over, he saw four words in clear scripted writing. On the paper were words, "You must find Elizabeth". What? Who the hell is

Elizabeth, and why is this in my boat? It wasn't there before. He gave the paper one last look and jammed it into his pants pocket as he reached his truck and climbed in.

When Daniel had been killed, he was residing in California. His body had unceremoniously been shipped back to Mississippi for burial. No one ever sent condolences, cards, or flowers, just the paperwork from the San Diego funeral home and a requested police report. It was as though life had simply swallowed him one night and nothing was left but memories. The driver had received a slap on the wrist, paid a lousy drunk driving fine, spent two weeks in jail and was out again living his life as though nothing had happened. Daniel was buried at the local Tarlton cemetery, and life kept spinning its daily routine, but for George and Eva time slowed to a crawl.

George took out the paper again and turned it over in his hands, as he sat befuddled in the truck. He realized he was sweating, but he didn't know why. It was a cool day for a change. Something in his heart had stirred when he read those words. Common sense told him it was just a piece of garbage, but some way he knew this was important. But where did thishis come from? Who wrote it? And he spoke the word on the paper again, as if for the first time. "You must find Elizabeth."

He went back to his house and crawled to his couch. He was suddenly exhausted, and fell into a deep disturbing sleep where he had strange dreams that he couldn't remember on waking. "What do I do" he prayed to whomever or whatever might listen.

George suddenly, desperately wanted to see his son's face again. The son he had known in a better life. He wanted to see Daniel's smile as he was in this life, happy, eyes sparkling and mischievous, filled with love for everyone. How had they come to be so far apart, in so many ways? This was his heart. He went to the desk and pulled out the last package of photos that were still in the rumpled paper folder in which they had been brought home from Wal Mart. He hadn't seen them for years now.

As he looked at each photo of Daniel smiling back at him, of Daniel and Eva, of himself and Eva and neighbors whose faces he had now almost forgotten, he smiled. Though tears stung his eyes, again, he filled up with all the memories he could pack into his head and heart for a day and began to put the photos back into the paper sleeve. When he went to put them back in the desk drawer, the drawer wouldn't close back so he had to shuffle things around. Somehow his hand found the folder in the corner of the drawer and as he picked it up to move it to make more room, the contents inside the folder shifted, causing him to drop everything on the floor. Papers and misery spilled out everywhere. It was the police report he never got around to reading. The trauma at the time, and the sorrow had kept these things at bay. Besides he knew the complete story by heart. But for some reason as he picked up all the pieces of Daniel's life from the floor, his eyes were drawn to the report. "Just damn". He didn't want to read it, but for some reason, he began reading. About halfway through the first page there was a report where the deceased body had been taken to the hospital and the passenger was transported to Scripp's hospital. "What passenger" thought George? No one had ever mentioned a passenger! A passenger!

George went to the phone, dialed his private eye friend Mason from a lifetime ago and called in a favor. Mason, this is going to sound crazy, but can you help me with a few details on something? I need to know about a passenger that was in Daniel's car when he died. George explained about the old report and gave his friend some details he need from the report to begin his search. Mason was just as surprised as George. Mason said it had been a long time, and it would take him some time and digging, but that he thought he could find what George was looking for. George said he just wanted to know who was in the car with Daniel when he died, and would be grateful for anything he could find.

Why was he just now finding out about this! Why didn't he keep up with things? He was both angry and excited and thinking he might hear about Daniel's last hours. He knew it was a long shot, but if anyone could help him it would be Mason.

The next few days passed slowly. George kept going over and over everything trying to make sense of what had happened or not happened to him. One moment he would decide he was off his rocker. The next he believed with all his heart he had experienced something divine.

On the third day, the phone rang and it was Mason calling him with his report. He had traced the passenger to a small town in California. “I have good news and bad news George.” Mason said somberly. The good news is the passenger was a woman, Brigitte Isabel Mercier, of French descent. The bad news is she died of cancer a while back in a San Diego hospital. George’s heart sank. There was actually an old detective at the station that remembered the wreck, as it had been down by the harbor where he fished off the pier a lot in his free time. He said he thought he remembered the girl in the car lived with the man.

That’s not quite all George. She had a young daughter, Elizabeth Danielle Mercier. She is her only survivor and is currently in foster care in southern California. That’s all I could dig up except the cemetery where Isabel is buried. Sorry George, not a lot of information.

Elizabeth ! How old is Elizabeth, Mason? Well, the time would correspond to the wreck. She must have been pregnant when Daniel was killed. George’s knees suddenly got weak and he had to sit down. I think she’s about twelve George. So where do we go from here?

I’ll hire you to go to California if you will. Mason said he had a couple of things to clear up here first, but that he would go. You know George, I loved that boy of yours too. A week passed before Mason could go to San Diego. George couldn’t sit still the whole week. He even started cleaning out the horrible mess he had made in the house. Cleaning something that hadn't been touched in months turned out to be quite a chore, but he did it slowly day by day and it made him feel better. He was on the home stretch of having a clean house.

In a small town in southern California, a young girl was sitting alone on a couch. She was what they used to call a latch key kid. She was only twelve, well almost thirteen now, but the life she had lived in those years made her feel like she was twenty. And that was old!

Elizabeth, was a child of the foster care system and was working on home number four. Why had her mother had to die and leave her all alone? It wasn't fair. The first home she had been in was not bad. The family seemed to care about her, but the father lost his job and the wife had become pregnant with their own children, twins, so they just couldn't do it financially any more, even with the money they were given to take care of her. When she went back in the system, it went downhill from there. The family she was with now had a monster of a son who was theirs. He got everything. She got nothing. They basically kept her for her monthly income to them and expected her to work at grownup things they should be doing. She had to go cook dinner now, as the lady would be home from her job at a convenience store soon and there would be dire consequences if her dinner wasn't perfect. The husband stayed gone most of the time, but when he did come in, he would drink beer until her passed out somewhere and God help you if you disturbed him. And Jeffery, the holy terror of a foster brother, bullied her every chance he got and ordered her around like she was scum on his show. When parents were around though, he grew angel wings for them. Elizabeth set about trying to cook dinner. She was learning quickly how to please, but inside she was getting numb.

Mason had made it to San Diego and had started off the morning running down a couple of leads he had. The second one panned out, as he found the girl he was looking for had been in foster care for five years now. He shook his head as he knew the odds weren't good of staying stable in the system. He also took the afternoon to drive to the cemetery on record for the mother. It was a small cemetery about twenty miles away but was worth the visit. When he finally found the grave, he was astonished as the headstone read Brigitte Isabel Mercier-Mavis. Mason almost dropped his phone as he took a picture of the headstone and sent it straight to George's text. The date she died had been nine years ago so that would add up to the child in foster care being twelve or thirteen. Mason breathed a heavy sigh. He wondered now how George wanted to proceed. What could he do?

The first thing that came to mind was a good lawyer.

George's phone buzzed. It startled him at first as he was in deep thought and wasn't used to many folks ever calling or texting him. He looked down and opened the text from Mason. His breath left him momentarily when he saw the picture. Isabel was Daniel's wife! Was Elizabeth really his grandchild? Oh God. He instantly replayed all the events that led up to this moment. Oh God, thank you. What do I do now, he prayed.

He didn't know how he knew, but he knew Elizabeth was his grandchild, just as he knew he had eaten that Twinkie in the boat. And how his heart did a flip flop when he uncrumpled that piece of paper from the boat. They were all leading him! George sent up a prayer again. His next earthly thought, a good lawyer. And then, where is she? So many questions filled his mind that he thought he would explode. He had to get to California, but he had to go talk to a lawyer first, and he knew just where he was going.

The lawyer was Conner Davis. Conner was an old family friend and had been in practice for twenty-something years. His specialty wasn't Department of Human Services or foster care, but he knew his way around and had a friend who was a specialist in that field. The two of them would work together, gather all the information they could find, including locating Elizabeth somehow, and make a plan.

Was there a plan to bring her to Mississippi? George honestly hadn't thought that far ahead. Could he take care of a teenager at his age? More questions. But he knew he was going to try to find the right answers for her. After all, maybe she was with a family that truly loved her. Maybe she was happy. But a nagging feeling from somewhere inside told him that wasn't true and that only a rescue would do. Conner advised him not to get too hasty in his actions that foster care had all the power right now and would come down hard. George didn't want to hear that but he took it to heart.

George was on a plane by early afternoon. He met with Mason at the airport and they decided to stay in the same hotel. They decided later to simply make it a suite, as it was still cheaper than two regular rooms and they both had plenty of space.

Mason had already managed to track down a marriage certificate which explained why Daniel hadn't told him anything about getting married. They had only been married a couple of weeks before the wreck, but from interviews from a couple of people that remained living in their area, Mason learned they had been together for a couple of years.

Next stop was Daniel's former employer. It was a long shot, like the latter interviews, but they had gained a little bit of information and after all these years every little bit counted. Daniel had been, of all things, a marine biologist. It was a little odd for a boy from Mississippi, but he had always had a love for the ocean, and when he was younger, he was on the Gulf coast at every opportunity. And when he got a taste of the ocean in California, that was where he wanted to be. It broke George's heart his son was so far away, but he was a grown man now. That was when he still had Eva. Oh, how he missed her.

There were a couple of people at Scripps Institute of Oceanography that still remembered Daniel. One was a guy he was on a project with for six months and they got to be pretty good friends, John said that Daniel was a great person and a top notch biologist. He had met Isabel and said that she and Daniel were so in love. He said it broke his heart when Daniel died. The other person was a supervisor and just remembered him being a good employee. But that was a start. It was late in the day by now, almost dark and George and Mason decided to go eat and just relax for a bit. They had a big seafood dinner and went back to the hotel and watched some tv and a few YouTubes. They were both exhausted and before they knew it, both were snoozing in their chairs. When they woke up from their respective naps, they went to their quarters and nodded out.

George was awakened in the morning by his phone. It was still early in California, but the day started long ago in the central time zone. "Hello." was all George could get out. It was Conner. Sending you a picture in your text George. Talk to you again in a bit. He thought that was a quick conversation. But when he opened the text, all became clear.

Staring back at him on his phone was the most beautiful little girl he had ever seen. Her hair was golden, her eyes were brown and she had beautiful olive skin. She looked like a little angel. Below the photo, it said, "Elizabeth, age 10." That would have been at least two years ago. How his heart ached. He had to see her. And she has Eva's eyes he said to himself. He got up, got dressed and showed the photo to Mason. They had a quick breakfast and headed out. They went to Scripp's hospital to see if they could find out any more about Isabel, but it was pretty much a dead end. They also made a stop at the San Diego Police Headquarters to see if there was any more information on Daniel's wreck. The folks were really friendly and sympathetic and went into storage to look for anything they might have. They did find a folder. It contained a copy of the same report George had at home, but it had one other thing, a few photos They asked George if he was sure he wanted to see them. He nodded. The car was a mangled scrap of raw metal. How could anyone survive that? The last photo was of a beautiful woman with blood all over her face. She had the same beautiful olive skin as Elizabeth. There were no pictures here of Daniel and he did not ask. Suddenly, George remembered something. When he was in that beautiful place with Eva and Daniel, a pretty girl had been talking to Daniel. He had already seen this beautiful face. It was Isabel and she was with Daniel, where ever they were, they were together. He longed to be with them, but now there was Elizabeth.

The phone rang again as they were leaving the station and it was Conner calling back. It was noon in San Diego, but about closing time in Tarlton. You might want to sit down for this George. You have an appointment at DHS in the morning at ten. They are in charge of foster care in Elizabeth's case and are going to assign someone to talk with you. This is about grandparent's rights. And look your best. You can bet you are being judged.

The night passed rather quietly. The two men went downstairs to the hotel bar to have a beer, but soon decided they were tired and hungry. Neither wanted to go out to eat, or eat in the hotel, so they ordered out for some Mexican food and had it sent to the hotel room. The food was awesome, and it was much more relaxing.

Morning came early. George was already up and dressed when Mason finally awoke. He was so nervous and had tried on two different outfits trying to feel comfortable with the task at hand. Soon, after some much needed coffee and a doughnut, they were on their way to the meeting. George wondered how Elizabeth's morning was going where ever she happened to be. Then it really hit him that he was in the city where his granddaughter was! He just needed to find her.

DHS, The Department of Human Services, California Social Services, Child Welfare System, Foster Care. So many names and individual agencies, it was overwhelming. When they arrived at the address they had been given, they weren't sure quite where to go. But they went to a desk at the front and were told they had to check in. So, they did.

About thirty minutes later a large woman came down the hall to meet them. She apologized for the delay but never explained. George was just ready to begin. The social worker was Sarah Johnson and she had been working in this area for ten years. She said she was the worker assigned to Elizabeth Mavis. Before either George or Mason could ask the first question she blurted out," Why have you waited all this time to contact us about this child? They were a bit shocked by her question, but George began answering immediately before he happened to remember his lawyer's warning about being careful about what he said. He finished answering, not providing many details. He explained that he had only recently learned of Elizabeth and the death of her mother and he wanted to be in Elizabeth's life.

The social worker frowned, whether she meant to or not. George noticed and said," I am her grandfather." Well, Mr. Mavis it's complicated. She's in her fourth home in five years. We just got her resettled not too long ago and we don't want to intrude on her situation. "Intrude on her situation?" George repeated. Just how do you want to be in her life Mr. Mavis? I don't mean to be crass, but how can you contribute to making her life healthy and happy? And you are older She is just a child. I can arrange for you to see her, but that's all I can promise at this time. George was livid as this was not what he was expecting at all, but he kept calm and simply said, "I'll take it." Are you currently staying in San Diego, asked Sarah? "Yes," he replied. "We'll have to meet at a neutral location, it's policy," she remarked." "What ever," replied George, "just do it." With that they were told they would be notified of a time and place. The two men left and were silent all the way back to the car.

George was on the phone to Conner before they left the parking area. The lawyer said that actually he had done just the right thing, to have the meeting and see what happened. Meanwhile, if the girl was in the mood tocome to Mississippi to live eventually, he was working on all the legalities of that. Conner reminded him to take one step at a time. Remember George, she doesn't even know about you yet. George sighed, he was right. And what if she doesn't want me?

Elizabeth's day had not gone well. She had a math test at school that she didn't even get to study for. She made a F on it, and that was awful as she was an A student. Her foster brother, Jeffrey had made her write a paper for him for school last night or threatened she would regret it big time if she didn't do it. He also said he would tear up her few personal items she had left of her former life, one of which was the only picture she had of her mother. She stayed up until three in the morning, but he got his stupid paper. He smirked when she handed it to him. "Good choice," he said.

Also, the foster father was on a total binge this week. Why didn't anyone ever check in on these people she thought to herself.

Tonight, the whole family was at home. This was starting to feel like one of the other homes she had been in where the foster care people had been called and they quickly pulled her out of that family. That father was now in prison for some crime he had committed while she was living with them.

She had just overheard a conversation she didn't quite understand about a man coming from Mississippi and demanding to see her. Who could that be? Her father was born in Mississippi, but he was dead. End of story. Mother told me how much she loved him and that he would have loved me so much. She talked about him a lot before she died. Damn car wrecks and damn cancer, she really couldn't think about all that right now, she just wanted to get out of this mess before it got really bad. She had become increasingly worried in the past few days, and she usually read people and situations pretty well for her young age. Tuesday, her question was answered.

Late Monday, the social worker, Sarah called. There would be a meeting tomorrow at Balboa Park. There were several areas in the park they could meet. The guys were to be at the entrance at two o'clock and don't be late.She would have Elizabeth with her, and they would be alone. The family supposedly had to work and couldn't get off. Elizabeth had been told she had a grandfather. She wasn't sure how to take the news or what he could possibly want to talk to her about. But it looked like she didn't have a choice and this would be better than being at that house.

Tuesday. Balboa Park. It was 2 p.m. George sat on a bench and could hardly breathe. Suddenly, he saw them. The matronly Sarah and a young girl that to him shone like the sun. She was even more beautiful than her picture. They saw him on the bench and walked over.

Elizabeth started the conversation, "Are you really my granddad?" "Yes, I am," said George. "My dad died before I was born. Why do you want to talk to me?" said the girl. I want to talk to you because you are my granddaughter, and I loved my son very much, and I love you even though we have never met, because you are a part of him and your sweet mother. There is so much I want to say to you, but I don't know where to start. I know this is the first time I've seen you but I didn't even know about you until a few weeks ago. I came as soon as I knew. Something was clicking between them. Would you mind if I gave you a hug? No one since her mom had ever offered that, so she walked over to George and they hugged each other. Elizabeth stepped back and asked him what did her want from her. And George just told her. I would love for you to come live with me in Mississippi. I don't have a lot, but I have a house, and we could get a dog and you would always have family that loved you. Sarah gasped. She wasn't expecting this from the old man.

Elizabeth was a bit shocked too, for a different reason. Could this be a real chance for a real family? But he was just an old man. She was so confused. I think that's enough for today you two. We need to get you home. Elizabeth turned and looked at him all the way to Sarah's car.

George tried to hold it together, but he started crying like a baby. She saw him crying, and then she started crying and the tears wouldn't stop. All of it sat on her. Her mom dying, all those mean people who had said they cared about her. It had all been bottled up and it all came sliding out.

Back at the house, the social worker had called her home, her foster mom was home already. Panic set in. His truck was in the driveway too. When she walked in it was quiz time. They wanted to know everything. After all, they had money on the line and hopes of getting a second kid to mooch off of. They told her she was to have nothing else to do with that man. And when Elizabeth said but he was her grandfather, the man turned around and slapped her so hard across the face she stumbled backwards and hit the nearby wall.. We are the only family you will ever have now, and don't forget it missy. She ran to her room, but standing in the door was monster

Jeff. He snarled and laughed at her. Elizabeth was in full panic mode but she had to stay calm until she could get out of the house.

She acted like she was over it all in the morning and went to school. When she got there, she went to the principal's office and asked to talk to the school social worker. That worker called Sarah. Sarah drove to the school and she and Elizabeth had a long talk,Sarah saw the bruise on Elizabeth's face. "I can't go back there; please don't make me go back there, help me."

I'm going to ask you a question now Elizabeth, and think hard about it before you answer. If you had a choice on what you would like to happen right now, what would it be? " "That's easy. Get my few things from that house and send me somewhere else." she replied. And what if this happens again in a new home?" asked Sarah "Then I'll just have to wait and see, won't I" I want to talk to my grandad!

"It's against my better judgment but we will call him right now". As it turned out the guys had gone to the pier at Mission Beach to walk off some of the crazy from yesterday. George almost dropped his phone in the water when he saw who was calling. Sarah said," A lot has happened since yesterday, and someone wants to talk to you. She handed Elizabeth the phone and it all came out again. I want to live with you grandad! George's heart nearly jumped out of his chest. Can I see you? Where are you? We are on our way. "You know I can get fired for this Lizzy?" said Sarah, but off to the beach they went anyway. It was a beautiful afternoon.

Sarah collected Elizabeth's few things as requested and said their foster would not be coming back. Things didn't happen immediately with the move and she had to stay elsewhere for about a month as everything worked its way through court. But Lizzy had turned thirteen and also pronounced where and with whom she wanted to live. The judge said okay to a living arrangement with a relative. That he believed it was in the best interest of the child to be with a blood relative. So that was that.

The day finally arrived and they all three flew back to Tarlton. When they got to the house she said, "I am home now." As George showed her everything, he took her to what used to be her father's room. There were boxes of stuff that remained of her father's life that George could never part with. She smiled so big. This will be my room, if it's okay, granddad. And the next day, they went out looking for a dog. They came home with two, and also a turtle she found in the yard. George thought I wonder where she got an idea like that?

That night, George dreamed again of the rest of his beautiful family that he knew without a doubt were together in heaven. He prayed for a long healthy life so he could be with the new light of his life. It all made sense now. Every word! “Thank you, God, I’ll try to get it right, ” he said as he rolled over and went back to sleep. I can’t wait for tomorrow.

Blue Toad's Blues

All the green toads were hurrying by, doing all the things that green toads do.

Blue Toad sat in the lily chair, by his mushroom table, munching on French fries with mustard, drinking a Pepsi with lots of ice, and wondering what all the fuss could be about. Other toads were scurrying about all over the pond, but he was content to just listen to his music. His headphones were own so load the music was spilling out everywhere around the surrounding pond. He just couldn't help it today though. This music was so beautiful, it made his heart sing with joy. He suddenly realized not only was his heart singing, so was his mouth, and quite loudly. No wonder he was getting strange looks. But that was okay. Nothing was going to spoil his peace today.

Blue Toad tried to be like all the other frogs, even though he was a deep blue. "Why couldn't I be green like everyone else" he mused? He always tried so hard, but he couldn't swim fast, or jump really high and he didn't look anything like the other frogs. He did love lying in the sun on warm rocks though. That was the best place to take frog naps or think.

Toad was also a bit chunky, a bit short and had strange hiccups. He squeaked when he had hiccups. And Toad was sprinkled with yellow sun spots. His mother used to call them frog freckles. He liked to wear the bright, yellow t-shirt that his friend Loki, the toucan had given him to help cover the spots. It wasn't so bad these days though. He was somewhat getting used to his looks. And anyway, every time he wore his shirt, the green frogs laughed at him. Life could be so embarrassing.

He just couldn't seem to fit into frog social circles. But that alone gave him lots of free time. Besides they ate flies at every outing, and oh, how he hated flies, yuk! He spit at the thought of them. French fries were so much better. He would keep trying to convince them.
time but no one could give him a good reason. All they could come up with was that he was different and they didn't like different. And he wondered why, oh why couldn't he be green?

But Blue Toad had a far worse frog sin. He loved to read, and think and debate. These things made his brain feel cool and stretchy. Many times, he thought about other things, wonderous things.

Blue Toad and Matea

He wondered what was on the other side of the great pond, and why the sky was so blue; where did the rain come from, and where did it go when the sun came out? Why made the sand so white? But then he would drift to the thing that puzzled him most. Why didn't the green toads like him. He asked one

Toad spent most of his days thinking and drawing and writing. He wrote stories and rhymes about the other frogs, mostly to try to understand them, and himself. Other days he would dream of going on an adventure across the great pond. He would lay on a warm flat rock for hours day-dreaming about all the stories he had heard. Loki had told him about the great blue oceans and the giant fishes that could eat a frog in one bite. That scared him a bit, but still he wished he could see these things for himself. Blue Toad was suddenly very lonely and longed with all his heart to see his dear friend.

In these days, Blue Toad became miserable. Many days, he cried big, blue tears. Only his dreams at night brought him peace. It was there in the quietness he dreamed he was a green frog. But when he awoke from those dreams, he always had a bad stomach ache and his head hurt. And always, when he awoke, he would still be blue. Once he even tried painting himself green, but as soon as he jumped into the water all the color washed away. Even Blue Toad thought this was a bit strange. But still he kept trying.

One morning Blue Toad awoke with a start after a long, fuzzy dream. He couldn't quite remember what happened, or what he was dreaming, but he felt different, and he felt good. His sadness was gone and had been replaced by total peace! His insides felt like the pond looked on a quiet morning when everyone was still asleep, cool and quiet, no ripples. Just this peaceful little feeling that was beginning to build inside of him, and made him want to dance all over the pond.

He felt strong. He felt deliriously happy. And then he realized he was singing to himself. And then, he started to dance on his little frog-toes. "Yippee, he shouted"

And then, it all came to him in a flash, flooding his mind instantly and making his universe orderly. I am a blue toad, and I will never be a green toad. Such a simple statement, but he had realized his worth. "How amazing" he thought. He wasn't at all sad, and never would be again. In fact, he was smiling. It was wonderful. With crystal clarity, Blue Toad knew that he was "Blue Toad" as things had been ordained. He was, as he was meant to be, by his creator. What a wonderful concept, he mused. "Oh, thank goodness" he said out loud. And then he thought about other things . . .

Now, he could eat his French fries with mustard, wear his yellow neon t-shirt, and listen to his beautiful opera. And maybe he would have friends over, maybe even some of the green frogs! Oh, and he must immediately get a message to Loki. He should be flying this way soon. And Matea, his beautiful, dusty-blue dragonfly friend. He hadn't seen her in a while. He
had to see them! I'm going to hop down the cove and find her right now. And off he went.

And some day, yes, some day for sure, and some day very soon, Blue Toad, Loki and Matea would visit the other side of the great pond!

Also by Joyce Burns

Life in the Pond
Thoughts on Moonlight, Ripples, Hearts and Frogs
A Collection of Poetry

Fragments
A Collection of Poetry

For more information visit:
www.chynablues.com
or email
chynablues13@gmail.com

PRESS©
chynablues

Nostalgic Rumination

When wisdom's berth has finally hit its mark,
and life is laid out straight along the road.
My days begin to fall like autumn leaves,
as winter's breath is laid across my soul.

I once was young, in youth without a care,
and spent my days and nights at reckless whim.
Just now I see the foolishness thereof,
as now I see my lights begin to dim.

'Tis true that life is wasted on the young,
but oh, what memories in hearts we keep.
Too soon this rose of life has passed away,
with nothing but our ashes in a heap.

So, drink the beauty of this bless-ed day,
for soon your perfect soul will fly away.

[1] A very special thanks to Charlotte Gray for the use of her quote on (p)08

www.ingramcontent.com/pod-product-compliance
Lightning Source LLC
LaVergne TN
LVHW010945100826
845153LV00002B/143

* 9 7 8 0 9 8 8 7 3 9 0 4 8 *